My Christmas Goose is almost Cooked

The Travel Mishaps of Caity Shaw
Book Three

❧ ☙

Eliza Watson

My Christmas Goose Is Almost Cooked

ISBN-10: 0-9992168-1-3
ISBN-13: 978-0-9992168-1-1

Printed in the United States of America.

Books by Eliza Watson

The Travel Mishaps of Caity Shaw Series

Flying by the Seat of My Knickers (Book 1)

Up the Seine Without a Paddle (Book 2)

My Christmas Goose Is Almost Cooked (Book 3)

Other Books

Kissing My Old Life Au Revoir

Writing Romance as Eliza Daly

Under Her Spell

Identity Crisis

Writing Young Adult as Beth Watson

Getting a Life, Even If You're Dead

To our Irish neighbors and friends
Des, Mags, and Darragh Carter

Thank you for the wonderful holiday memories and
for helping us to make our Ireland house a home.
And for the chicken curry...

ACKNOWLEDGMENTS

I cannot even begin to thank all of my Irish rellies and friends for including Mark and me in your holiday festivities and for sharing your family traditions. I've enjoyed tasting my first Christmas pudding, pulling my first cracker and wearing its crepe paper crown, and attending my first St. Stephen's Day celebration rather than fighting crowds hunting for after-Christmas bargains. Thanks a mil for making our holidays so memorable. I look forward to many more!

I would like to thank my husband, Mark, and all my friends and family for believing in me and supporting my writing in so many ways. I would have given up years ago without your encouragement. Thank you to Nikki Ford and Elizabeth Wright for your in-depth feedback, helping to make this a stronger book. Thanks to Sandra Watson for providing professional insight into narcissistic personality disorder and the damaging emotional effect narcissists have on their victims. To Judy Watson for reading the book numerous times. And to Laura Iding—if it wasn't for all of our brainstorming sessions over wine and dinner, I might still be plotting book one.

To Dori Harrell for your fab editorial skills and for always exceeding my expectations. To Chrissy Wolfe for your final proofreading tweaks. To Lyndsey Lewellen for another incredible cover and for capturing the spirit of Caity. And to Amy Atwell at Author E.M.S. for a flawless interior format and for always promptly answering my many questions.

Thanks to my brilliant fans, who began this adventure with Caity in *Flying by the Seat of My Knickers* and who continue to follow her journey around Europe!

My Coffey Family Tree

Cheat Sheet

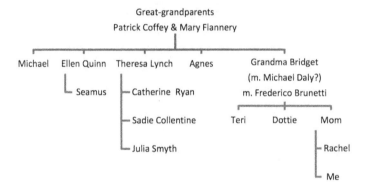

Great-grandparents
Patrick Coffey & Mary Flannery

| Michael | Ellen Quinn | Theresa Lynch | Agnes | Grandma Bridget |

Seamus

Catherine Ryan

Sadie Collentine

Julia Smyth

(m. Michael Daly?)

m. Frederico Brunetti

Teri   Dottie   Mom

Rachel

Me

CHAPTER ONE

"We're in trouble, Caity." Panic filled the older woman's voice on the other end of my cell phone.

"Bernice? What's wrong? Where are you?"

Bernice was a winner in Brecker beer's consumer promotion trip—Deck the Halls—to Dublin. Her sister, Gracie, was her guest.

"At some Christmas market. All the little shops look alike. Can't figure out how to get out of here and back to the hotel."

"Give a taxi driver the hotel's card."

"We don't have money for a taxi."

"They take credit cards."

"We don't believe in credit cards." Bernice gasped. "Oh dear, it's so loud and so many people!"

"I've seen that market. I'll be there in fifteen minutes."

I disconnected, heaving a frustrated groan, though I could sympathize, being directionally challenged myself. And my job as an event planner was to assist if any of the trip's twenty winners and their guests ended up missing, in the hospital, or in jail. Most of them had never been abroad and were even less travel savvy than me. Scary.

I called my sister, Rachel, Brecker's lead event planner, and explained that I was off to rescue Bernice and Gracie. She and my Irish coworker Declan were checking out a pub for future events.

Actually, six weeks ago Declan had become more than a *coworker*. We'd been kicked out of Paris's Musée d'Orsay for making out in the middle of the Impressionist wing. Not only wouldn't Rachel condone coworkers dating—or making out in an art museum— she'd wig out that I'd succumbed to Declan's playboy charms, despite her warning. Having recently confided in Rachel about my emotionally abusive ex-boyfriend, Andy, had helped mend our strained relationship. Her advice had been to avoid men and take time to find myself. I'd given myself the same advice before kissing Declan. It was stellar advice, but I wasn't listening to either one of us.

I was listening to my heart.

The Christmas market was a short walk from the Connelly Court Hotel. Steaming mulled wine and the scent of evergreen boughs, which decorated rows of wooden stalls, filled the unseasonably warm evening air. Vendors sold gingerbread houses with white and red icing, Christmas cakes and puddings, holiday crafts, and gifts. I found Bernice and Gracie in front of a pub's stand, dancing an Irish jig to "Feliz Navidad" playing over the sound system. They didn't look panicked or lost. The petite gray-haired women wore matching red Brecker sweatshirts and green Santa stocking caps with Flanagan's logo—a Dublin-based brewery owned by Brecker. I had on an identical sweatshirt and a Brecker scarf. Despite my auburn hair and pale skin, the right shade of red was a good color for me, unlike orange.

I slipped Brecker's camera from my purse and snapped a few pics of the women. I'd been promoted from wearing a foam sausage costume and posing with VIPs at the last Dublin meeting to company photographer, capturing candid shots of the winners for future promotional materials. I had to impress Rachel with some killer shots. No way was I being demoted to a sausage, one of my most humiliating experiences.

My gaze narrowed on the women. "You don't look lost."

"We thought you needed to get out and have some fun." Bernice nudged me with her elbow, encouraging me to sing along.

Gracie placed her Santa cap on my head. For the first time in three years, my seasonal employment hadn't required an elf hat. My Cheesey Eddie's uniform had included a foam cheesehead, though. The only thing that had made my elf gigs tolerable was singing Christmas carols.

I joined the women, belting out one of my favorite tunes. When the song ended, the ladies reached down for plastic cups containing a dark liquid. Bernice fished out a euro someone had tossed in her drink.

"What's that?" I asked.

"Mulled wine," Bernice said. "Don't cramp our style by drinking tea."

"I don't want a drink." I glanced around the busy market. "I need some gifts."

I had no idea what to buy Declan. I'd considered using my Cheesey Eddie's employee discount for a block of cheese shaped like Wisconsin. Nothing said we were just friends like a hunk of cheddar. Yet I didn't want to buy him something too intimate when we hadn't yet *been* intimate.

"If you entered contests, you wouldn't have to spend time Christmas shopping," Bernice said. "I'm giving my grandson an iPad I won."

"Hopefully, I win that riding lawn mower." Gracie crossed her fingers. "I'm downsizing my life and selling my car."

Bernice nodded. "Remember when I won that trip to London but Larry insisted we take the cash payout for a new car? Our car was just fine, but no arguing with the man when the entry form was from his case of beer." She raised her glass. "Here's to Larry and Irvin. May they rest in peace." The ladies took swigs of their wine. "And to Scotland next year, homeland of our McKinneys."

Gracie smiled wide. "Oh my yes, to men in kilts."

These women sounded like their husbands' *deaths* were the beginning of their *lives*.

"How do you learn about all of these contests?" I asked.

Attendees had won this all-expense paid trip to Dublin by submitting a one-thousand-word essay to Brecker's marketing department, describing their favorite memories involving the beer. Bernice's story included a vintage Brecker tray her grandmother had used to serve Christmas cookies and snacks at family gatherings, including Bernice's high school graduation. Her mother continued the tradition, and they'd passed Brecker beer on it at Bernice's father's funeral. I'd teared up when Rachel had me read the entry.

"Contests are everywhere on social media," Gracie said. "And forums, which are also a great way to meet men. I met an Irish gent, and we're hooking up with him and his friend tonight. Better than a dating site."

"You never know where you'll meet a guy," Bernice said with a wink.

A man in a red jacket and green wool cap stood on a stage in an open square. A backdrop of sponsor banners included Guinness, Jameson, and Tayto—Ireland's delicious potato chips. The crowd's lively chatter faded to a hush.

"It's time to announce the next winner in our silent auction benefiting Ireland's Hospice Foundation. The winner for Christmas Cuisine with Finn O'Brien, is... Caity Shaw."

"What the hell?" I muttered, my gaze darting to Bernice and Gracie eagerly pointing me out to the curious crowd. "*This* was why you wanted me here?"

"Our sister Clara just passed away from cancer and was in hospice." Bernice frowned. "We'd been trying to think of a way to memorialize her this Christmas."

"But why'd you sign *my* name?"

"If only I were ten years younger..." Bernice gazed longingly through a glassy-eyed haze at the tall, handsome dark-haired guy walking up on stage.

"I can't go on a date with this guy."

"It's not a date," Gracie said. "He's a famous Irish chef. You get to cook in his restaurant with him."

My eyes widened. "That's even *worse*."

I'd once broiled banana bread instead of baking it. When I'd sawed into the brick-like loaf, it'd oozed batter. On three occasions, I'd set kitchen towels on fire. And who'd have thought that recycled wax paper could ignite in a microwave?

"He'll do all the cooking." Bernice waved away my concern. "Besides, he's one of Dublin's most eligible bachelors."

Gracie leaned in, lowering her voice. "Actually, he was the most eligible bachelor *last* year and is number three this year, so we got him for a steal. He's a hottie, though, isn't he?"

What happened to it not being a date?

Finn peered over at me, along with the spectators, undoubtedly wondering why I was hesitant to claim my prize. The sisters gave me a shove, and I stumbled forward. I shot them an annoyed glance. The crowd parted, opening a path for me. I walked up on stage and nodded hello to Finn. I had to set him straight that I wasn't completely desperate, bidding on some random man in an auction. I was also a serious fire hazard.

"Congratulations." The announcer shook my hand. "This is every cook's dream come true, lessons from Finn O'Brien."

I nodded faintly, staring nervously at the crowd, whereas Finn looked comfortable with the attention.

"Can you give us a *taste* of what your menu will entail?" The announcer laughed at his joke, handing Finn the microphone.

"We're going to prepare a traditional Irish Christmas dinner with my secret recipe for goose."

People ate goose?

"Kiss her!" a weirdo guy yelled out.

With an amused smile, Finn slipped his hand around mine, raised it to his mouth, and placed a warm kiss against it. He lowered my hand, giving it a reassuring squeeze to put me at ease.

My chest fluttered. Not from Finn's kiss but at Declan's blue Irish eyes staring curiously up at me from in front of the stage. He quirked a questioning brow. My gaze darted to Bernice, Gracie, and Rachel, standing next to him.

Sweating, I loosened the scarf around my neck. I didn't know who was going to be more upset, Declan or Rachel. When we'd left Paris, Declan and I'd never agreed not to date other people. I wasn't sure *what* we'd agreed to. And Rachel would be ticked I was wasting money bidding on this guy when I was massively in debt and always begging her for contract work. My only future job was a February meeting in Venice for the planner I'd worked with in Paris.

I gave the crowd a little wave and bolted off stage, Finn trailing down the steps behind me. My entourage met me at the bottom of the stairs.

"So what else are you cooking besides goose?" Bernice took a pic of the chef flashing a charismatic smile, something he likely did on a regular basis for the media and the mirror.

Finn's awareness of his effect on women was apparent in his confident smile, relaxed stance, and fleeting glances at his admirers. Declan was receiving his share of stares too. However, he oozed sex appeal without effort, or currently even a smile. He raked a disinterested hand through his short, wavy brown hair, and a clump fell across his forehead. His dreamy blue eyes weren't skittering around checking out women. They were fixed on me, making me sweat even more.

"Dinner is a surprise," Finn said.

"Oh really?" Bernice gave him a suggestive grin.

I avoided Declan's gaze.

Was he waiting for me to inform Finn that we were dating? Technically, we weren't. Even if we were, I couldn't admit it in front of Rachel.

My sister introduced herself to Finn. She had on a stylish red knit cap over her brown hair, a red wool jacket, and the Brecker scarf. Her red lipstick tied her outfit together. "This is such a great cause you're donating your time to."

Finn smiled at me. "It's very generous of *Caity* to donate money to tonight's auction. Thanks a mil for that."

"She does charity stuff all the time," Gracie said.

"Something you two have in common." Bernice winked at him.

"How's the show going?" Declan asked Finn. Head tilted to the side, he rubbed a curious hand over his five o'clock shadow.

The chef's confident smile wavered. "Ah, no longer doing it."

"Oh, too bad." Declan's smug look said he'd known damn well the show was off.

"What show?" Rachel asked.

"Finn was a judge on one of those reality TV cooking

shows here in Ireland," Bernice said. "We read it in his profile."

"Nice." Rachel nodded, clearly impressed.

I gave Finn an apologetic smile. "I'm only in town two more days, and I have to work tomorrow night. Maybe Bernice and Gracie could take my place."

"You can have off," Rachel said. "There's not much going on."

Since when?

"Grand." Finn handed me his business card. "Ring me tomorrow, and I'll give you the details."

Bernice held up her empty cup. "We'll be by your restaurant's stand for more wine."

Finn paused briefly for a picture with two patiently waiting fans, then strode off, a trail of women casually stalking him.

"We need to go also." Gracie snatched her Santa cap from my head. "Don't want to be late for *our* dates."

"He isn't a date," I yelled out as the ladies left. I turned to Rachel and Declan. "I didn't bid on this guy. Gracie and Bernice did, in memory of their sister, and put my name on it. I have no clue who he is."

"His family owns O'Brien's restaurants," Declan said.

Rachel's blue eyes widened. "As in *James* O'Brien?"

Declan nodded reluctantly. "His dad."

Rachel bubbled with enthusiasm. She was so not the bubbly type. "Excellent. Finn O'Brien has grown their family business to ten restaurants in Ireland. They don't carry Brecker Dark, only Flanagan's cider ale. This is a great opportunity to get Brecker in there."

My gaze narrowed. "So you're pimping me out to get more business?"

"He's doing this for the publicity, not to find a woman."

"He's doing it for both, as usual," Declan said.

"It's business," Rachel said. "And it couldn't have worked out better if I'd planned it."

Rachel *hadn't* planned it, *had* she? This was precisely something Rachel would do to land more business and earn brownie points with Brecker's CEO, Tom Reynolds. However, she looked genuinely surprised about Finn's identity.

"What am I supposed to do? If he asks if I'd like a drink, I request Brecker Dark? Then when he says they don't have it, I whip out your business card? That won't be obvious at all."

"Just casually mention why you're in town and segue into it. This is even better than your pub-crawl idea."

In Paris, I'd given an Irish pub's bartender Rachel's card. The place now carried Brecker Dark. This had inspired me to pub hop in Dublin, ordering Brecker Dark and recommending the beer if the pub didn't carry it. An added bonus, Declan and I could sneak off to out-of-the-way pubs and make out like a normal couple, without being paranoid about Rachel catching us.

Developing the marketing plan on my own had been a pivotal point in my career, giving me a glimmer of hope that I might *have* a career after being fired from my office job six months ago.

"I can't cook," I said. "The kitchen is not my friend."

"You were like twelve when you went to the emergency room over that bagel incident."

I hadn't even remembered I'd sliced my finger cutting a bagel! I massaged the faint scar on my thumb.

Dressing in an apron could prove even more embarrassing than dressing up like a sausage. I had to draw the line at cooking. However, that *line* was hazy and getting even blurrier the less work I had. The instability of this job was nerve-racking, especially when self-employment taxes were looming in my financially bleak future.

Just how far would I have to go to keep this job?

CHAPTER
TWO

Rachel disappeared into the crowd, and Declan snatched Finn's card from my hand. "I can't believe that wanker kissed you, playing to the crowd."

"It was on the hand and for a good cause." I grabbed the card back.

"Yeah, to feed his ego. He shags every woman who walks into his restaurant. And the food's total rubbish."

"You think I'd let this guy shag *me*?"

Declan hadn't even shagged me. By my choice.

"No...of course not."

What was with the hesitation? *I* should be the one not trusting *him*. God only knew how many women Declan had slept with since his wife, Shauna, had died three years ago.

I'd nicknamed his women Guinness Girls because alcohol had likely played a role with several. However, I trusted that he hadn't slept with anyone since our first kiss.

Declan grasped hold of my hand. Just shy of kissing

it, he peered at me through thick lashes, a mischievous glint in his blue eyes. "I want more than your hand."

He whisked me into the dark shadows behind the stands and warmed my lips with his. I returned his kiss and melted against him, letting out a faint moan. Declan was only a half foot taller than me, around five feet nine inches, so our bodies molded perfectly together. I curled my fingers into his soft blue wool sweater, wanting to run them through his hair so his rain-scented shampoo would linger on my skin...

I finally mustered up the resistance and drew back, breathing heavily, puffs of steam floating from my mouth. I glanced around.

Declan's smile faded. "Don't worry. Rachel's gone."

"I don't want us to lose work because she's afraid us dating will get in the way of our jobs. We need to prove it won't before I tell her. Not just because of the money, but I'd never see you." Declan was booked solid until the end of February. Between trips, he planned to pop over to Venice for a day so we could squeeze in a romantic dinner and gondola ride. "And I've been killing myself to prove to Rachel I can handle this job. No way can I not do this cooking gig."

And Rachel thinks you're a total player.

Declan released my hand, and it slipped from his, dropping to my side. "You're right. You need to do it. You'll be grand."

Seriously? He hadn't put up much of a fuss.

A fact I should appreciate, since I'd overreacted a few times when his actions had reminded me of Andy's controlling behavior. However, I hadn't had a distressing Andy flashback since Declan and I kissed.

My thoughts had been focused on Declan. The only reason I'd gone to see my counselor, Martha, after Paris was to tell her about the kiss and prove that I was starting to recover from post-traumatic stress disorder. I hadn't felt this positive about myself or a guy in a long time.

Declan held my gaze, an intense look in his eyes. "I trust you. The wanker just rubs me the wrong way."

And maybe Declan was a tad jealous? It was a flattering kind of jealousy, not a scary one, like Andy's had been.

He gave me a fleeting kiss, then stepped from the shadows, strolling over to a mulled wine stand. "My parents are mad about this stuff. I should get them some for Christmas."

That was the first thing I knew about Declan's parents. I knew more about Finn O'Brien's dad than I did Declan's.

Did his parents know anything about *me*?

Declan bought two cups of mulled wine. The steam warmed my cheeks, and the scent of cinnamon filled my nose. I took a sip. Delish. At least his parents and I shared a love for mulled wine. Declan bought a few bottles, and we headed to a gingerbread stand.

"Maybe I should bring Sadie Collentine a gingerbread house. Our family photo and the letters her mom wrote my grandma aren't really a *gift*."

Following this program, Rachel and I were going to meet our newfound rellie in Killybog, County Westmeath. Until recently, I hadn't known that Grandma Brunetti, née Coffey, had been from Ireland. Sadie's response to my letter had been vague. I was hoping she could provide answers to Grandma's mysterious past. Like the fact that she might have been previously married in Ireland before immigrating to the US in 1936.

I admired the fancy gingerbread houses decorated in red and white icing. "They look too perfect to eat."

"My granny's gingerbread houses looked more like deserted Irish dwellings. Slanted walls, crooked roofs, and a bit dilapidated. Drinking her homemade cider while constructing them didn't help. One year, the top blew off an unopened bottle, spraying the gingerbread houses and kitchen with sticky apple cider. It was a bloody mess, but my granny kept on decorating. The houses tasted brilliant, and everyone wanted her recipe. I was the only one who knew her secret."

As usual, Declan's story had me giggling.

"Which grandma?" I asked.

"Granny Byrnes, my mum's mum, who passed away last year. The one whose father ran off with the pastor's wife and I sent postcards to when traveling."

Outside of Declan's grandma, I knew little about his family. Except that they lived a half hour from my rellie Sadie Collentine in Killybog, and his parents were currently visiting his mom's sister in Waterford. Also, his sister, Zoe, loved Halloween, and she'd once gotten a splinter in her butt while sliding down a wooden banister. I was Facebook friends with her, but she rarely posted. She commented on Declan's posts, but he'd avoided Facebook since I'd tagged him in Paris and a psycho ex-Guinness Girl had stalked us.

"Is your grandma Grady still alive?"

He nodded.

Did she live near his parents? *With* his parents? How was her health? He always gave the briefest answers possible when it came to his personal life, unless it entailed a humorous story of his past shenanigans or work mishaps. Declan admitting he'd been avoiding his feelings since Shauna's death had prompted our kiss in Paris. I'd hoped he'd continue opening up. If not about Shauna, about his family.

A narcissistic jerk demeaning his wife at the Palace of Versailles had forced me to confront my demons and to slowly start confiding in Declan about Andy.

I had to be patient. At least he hadn't claimed his entire family was dead to avoid discussing them, like Grandma Brunetti had. I was likely the first "steady" girlfriend he'd had since Shauna. I didn't expect him to forget about Shauna or to stop wearing his bracelet—a braided brown leather band with a silver Celtic design of interloping knots symbolizing everlasting love. His love for Shauna, no doubt. Our relationship was a big step forward for Declan. A big step for me. After my brutal breakup with Andy six months ago, I never thought I'd ever even kiss another guy. The only reason I hadn't done *more* than kiss Declan was that I needed to know where our relationship was going. The fact that Declan respected this made me respect him even more.

Declan and I entered the Connelly Court Hotel, greeted by a towering tree with twinkling red lights in the middle of the marble-floored lobby. A lively Celtic Christmas tune made me want to step dance despite not having international health insurance to cover a broken ankle. The aroma of warm cedarwood with a hint of cinnamon replaced the hotel's signature vanilla lavender scent. The gift shop sold the calming scent in the forms of a candle, diffuser, or spray so you could enjoy it at home. I didn't see how waking up to a reminder of the Connelly Court Hotel would reduce my stress. My first meeting here had been one mortifying mishap after another—pilfering items from an expensive gift basket I'd thought was mine and falling flat on my face in front of Brecker's CEO.

Evergreen boughs with red bows framed the elevator doors. We stepped into one with an older couple dressed in elegant evening attire. The lady admired Sadie's gingerbread house while her husband pushed the button for floor three. Declan pushed twelve. Neither of our rooms were located on floor twelve. I gave him a questioning glance. He responded with a sly grin. The couple exited on the next floor, and the doors slid shut. Declan slipped his arms around my waist, drawing me snugly against him, planting his lips on mine. When we reached the twelfth floor, I was out of breath, my body on fire. Nobody joined us, so Declan sent the elevator back down. The doors closed, and we were once again all over each other.

It was late. We could probably ride the elevator alone until I got motion sickness. Or we could go to one of our rooms. I'd been in Declan's room several times prior to our first kiss, but not since then. That was how I'd learned his travel tips—whiskey was the best glass sanitizer and always store your TV remote in a plastic baggie.

Declan's phone vibrated against our waists, sending a tingling sensation throughout my thighs. Maybe I *was* ready for a physical relationship with Declan...

He grabbed his phone with an annoyed groan.

"Who's Aidan?" I couldn't help but see the name displayed on the screen.

"My brother in London."

I'd known about a brother in London but hadn't known his name.

Declan pushed floor six. "He's left several messages, making sure I'll be home for Christmas. I better ring him back."

Declan hadn't visited his family since Easter. Had he not gone home last Christmas?

The doors slid open, and Declan poked his head out. Coast clear, he ducked back in and gave me a quick kiss good night. He stepped out, holding the door. "Did I ever tell ya about the time I got stuck in a lift with a claustrophobic client?" He wore a teasing smile as the doors slid closed.

I couldn't believe he'd left me hanging!

Wearing a goofy grin, I inhaled the faint woodsy scent of Declan's cologne lingering in the air and on my Brecker scarf. I buried my nose in the knit fabric, relaxing against the wall.

Back in my room, I slipped the keycard in the slot by the door to activate the lights. After one last whiff, I tossed my scarf on the red throw draped across the bed's crisp white sheets. I'd stored the white duvet in the closet, unsure when it was last washed and afraid it might be a bit *dodgy*. Another Declan travel tip. A stuffed snowman with a shamrock on his red sweater—a gift from Rachel—sat on the nightstand next to the framed photo of Grandma and her sister Theresa—Sadie Collentine's mother. The photo was from 1935, the same era as a black-and-white Dublin street scene hanging over the headboard. I set Sadie's gingerbread house next to Grandma's picture.

Browsing through the Christmas market hadn't inspired any gift ideas for Declan. At least I had money to buy presents, thanks to sixty-hour workweeks at Cheesey Eddie's and a hefty check from my Paris program. I'd made a nice dent in my major credit card. Upon paying off my department store cards, I had cut them up in celebration. I still didn't have my own place to live, a car, or income taxes paid, and my student loan would be kicking in next month. My massive debt was another sad reminder of trying to live up to Andy's unrealistic expectations and flashy lifestyle.

Christmas was a time of perpetual hope.

Hopefully, I got some work pronto.

I pulled up my résumé on my laptop and added *Developing program marketing strategies.* It would likely be the only new update, since this was a no-brainer program. Not ideal when I needed to learn my job. However, I could now boast having worked consumer promotions in addition to VIP meetings and sales incentives.

I could also boast being a seasoned packer. Unlike previous trips, I hadn't forgotten socks, undies, or jammies. I threw on my pj's—an oversized green Coffey's Pub T-shirt—and red-and-green plaid leggings.

Last trip, Gerry Coffey, a Dublin bartender, had kindly given me the shirt off his back thanks to Rachel shamelessly flirting with him. She'd surprised us with dinner at our surname pub. His Coffey family tree was deeply rooted in County Cork, ours in County Westmeath. But who knew—maybe we were third cousins five times removed.

I propped my pillow against the headboard and slipped into bed with my travel journal. I opened to my list of firsts and added that I'd won my first guy in an auction and would have my first cooking experience with the famous chef. I'd started the list two months ago on my first trip abroad, with my first Guinness and my first castle, Malahide Castle. Thanks to the stupid cooking gig my final night in town, I could forget about crossing Dublin Castle off my bucket list.

My cell phone rang. Mom. I'd found an international calling plan within Brecker's allowable budget, so I answered my phone without freakin' over the cost.

"Should we have pigs in a blanket and bacon-wrapped wienies?" Mom asked. "I'm making out the grocery list."

I hadn't helped plan our annual Christmas Eve party the past two years. Last year I'd shown up with Andy and snooty catered appetizers, including liver pâté, which Uncle Benny had fed to a feral cat on our patio, thinking it was pet food. Furious, Andy had maintained his unflappable composure by popping the cork on a $137 bottle of champagne and bragging about the price. I'd been too brainwashed to be mortified by his arrogance. I was determined to make it up to Mom this year. I'd be arriving home the morning of the twenty-third, plenty of time to grocery shop and prepare food.

"Both sound delish," I said.

"I'll e-mail you the menu to see if I'm missing anything. And of course we'll have your delicious cheese balls, dip, and curds. Who knew Cheesey Eddie's sold so many varieties of curds. Only in Wisconsin. Of course, your father has already polished off the beer-flavored ones, so I scratched those from the list."

I about gagged at the thought of all that cheese. My temp job might have ruined cheese for me for life.

I didn't plan to tell Mom I might pick up some cooking tips from Finn O'Brien. She would fret about my past kitchen mishaps and make me even more nervous about it.

"Aunt Teri's baking your grandma's cookies this year."

Grandma Brunetti's Italian Pizzelle cookies were the best.

"I wonder if any of her cookies were Irish recipes," I said. "Maybe we've been carrying on a family tradition without even knowing."

Mom wasn't aware that Grandma's Ellis Island record noted her last name as Daly. I needed to confirm that the certificate I'd found online for a Bridget Coffey and Michael Daly, married in England, was indeed Grandma's. Not that Mom would care he'd been Protestant and not Catholic, though their families had likely cared a great deal. Mom cared that Grandma had been writing letters her entire life to her supposed dead sister in Ireland. I wanted Mom to have closure with her mother. However, I was beginning to fear my discoveries might make her resent her mother even more. The more I learned about the woman who'd died when I was only seven, the more I aspired to be like her. I admired her sense of courage and adventure. I wanted Mom to feel this same connection. I'd wait and see what Rachel and I uncovered in Killybog and drop the entire bomb at once.

I had a haunting feeling Sadie Collentine would be sharing dark family *secrets* rather than family *recipes*.

CHAPTER THREE

The following morning, I went down to the second floor to cross over to the elevators in our office wing. Declan had once taught me this trick to avoid the lobby and attendees' difficult questions. This trip, it was more to admire my favorite Christmas tree decorated with champagne-colored bows, gold ornaments, and a gold glittery tree skirt with...red tennies sticking out from underneath it.

What the hell?

Loud snoring and the stench of eau de whiskey filled the air. I peeked around the back of the tree to find familiar dark hair gelled into a wild frenzy, the guy's head weighing heavily on a gold-wrapped box. Omigod.

Curt. One of our attendees.

I certainly wouldn't be snapping a picture of this scene.

Thankfully, it was early and the executive office floor was deserted. Rachel would be livid if this idiot got kicked out of Brecker's and Flanagan's preferred

Dublin hotel. She'd be the one explaining it to the companies' CEOs and our hotel contact. I refused to call Declan, or Rachel, for help.

I could handle this.

I gave Curt's tennie a kick. A faint groan filled the air along with an even stronger smell of whiskey. I kicked his foot harder.

He grunted and tugged the tree skirt up to his chin, nestling into it. "Knock it off, Derik." His voice was raspy from cigarettes and booze.

"It's not Derik," I hissed. "Get up. Now." I gave him a kick to the shin this time.

He let out a yelp.

I yanked the tree skirt off him, but he snagged a corner and pulled it back over himself.

"Seriously, dude, knock it off."

"If you do not get up right now, I'm putting you on the next plane home at your own expense. And no more Jameson."

He squinted up at me. "You're not Derik."

"No kidding. But I *am* dead serious."

He rolled out from under the tree, wrapping the red skirt around his shoulders and his red Brecker T-shirt. I'd given Derik and him a half dozen extra shirts thinking it would be great promo for them to wear to the pubs.

Now, I wasn't so sure.

He managed to drag himself up, rocking back on his heels. I grabbed hold of his arm, steadying him, before he and the tree went timber.

He peered at the skirt wrapped around his shoulders. "Hey, I'm a superhero. Super Curt."

I grabbed the "cape" and put it back in place under the tree. I hid the crushed present in the corner behind.

"Do you have your room key?"

He nodded, wearing a suggestive smirk. "You wanna go back to my room?" He continued nodding. "Awesome." He checked his jeans pockets, coming up empty except for a euro, a few peanuts, and the label from a beer bottle. "Looks like we have to go to *your* room."

I rolled my eyes.

He'd blown away too many brain cells on this trip to even recall his room number, so I found it on the list in my binder. We waited for the elevator, Curt leaning an annoying arm against my shoulder. The elevator doors opened, and a group of hotel executives, dressed in black, exited. I recognized several from our hotel pre-con meeting, including the general manager. He held the door for us, unable to hide his curious stare, his top lip curling back from Curt's stench.

He smiled. "Having a good stay in Dublin?"

Curt was sniffing my hair.

I nodded earnestly. "Incredible. Everyone is raving about your hotel."

Curt drew his nose back from my head and slipped his arm around my shoulder. "Awesome hotel, dude. Can't wait to come back. You should give my chick a raise."

The doors slid shut on the manager's confused gaze.

We'd almost been home free.

"I don't work for the hotel, you idiot, and we're not dating." Fuming, I threw Curt's arm off my shoulder, and he stumbled back against the wall.

The door opened, and I grasped his elbow, propelling him off the elevator. I knocked on his guest room door. No answer. After pounding several times, Derik finally appeared, naked except for a pair of boxers with a frothy-topped pint of beer printed on them. I shoved Curt into the room and left them with a stern warning they would immediately forget.

I headed back toward the elevator, sniffing myself, deciding I reeked like a booze hag. I went to my room and exchanged my Brecker red-logoed white cotton shirt for an identical one hanging on the bathroom door. Hating to iron, I relied on the shower steam to remove the wrinkles. I threw on my black suit jacket and brushed on more Flirty Fuchsia lip gloss to brighten my boring outfit. I blasted my hair with hairspray to fumigate any lingering smell of Curt's whiskey breath.

I was almost a half hour late. Now avoiding the hotel offices on the second floor, I took the elevator down to the lobby. Bernice and Gracie strolled in the front entrance, wearing yesterday's clothes.

"What happens in Ireland, stays in Ireland." Bernice winked as they scurried over to catch the elevator.

Since we were still in Ireland, I was definitely telling Rachel about their contest-forum hookup. She'd need a laugh before I told her about Curt.

Maybe this program wasn't a no-brainer. It just required different skills than the three corporate meetings I'd worked. I was proud I'd handled Curt on my own without having to call Declan to help me haul his drunken ass up to his room.

I entered our staff office. The same one we'd had for

our October meeting. Working at a familiar hotel provided a sense of stability in our unpredictable event-planning world. You knew the layout, the staff's service level, if the minibars had sensors... A discovery I'd made at a Paris hotel when I'd been billed for a dozen diet sodas I'd never drank.

Rachel's plum-colored lips clashed with her red dress and nails. No jewelry accessorized her outfit. A major fashion faux pas for her. Rather than flat-ironing her wavy brown hair, the sides were pulled back in a clip. She never wore her hair back for work. I did all the time, preferring to sleep than to fuss with my hairstyle. At the rate her nails were flying across the keyboard, she'd already downed several energy drinks.

She gazed up from her computer, smiling despite her disheveled appearance.

I told her about the sisters.

She laughed. "That could be us in forty years."

That was more *scary* than it was *funny*. I feared we might end up spinsters, not widows.

I explained my tardiness was thanks to Curt.

"Glad *you* found the idiot." She polished off an energy drink and tossed the can in the garbage. "If these guys end up in the emergency room from alcohol poisoning, they're on their own."

An empty threat since she knew *we'd* be dealing with it.

She was taking the incident much more calmly than I'd expected, especially since she was wired on energy drinks. She obviously had a lot going on, so I decided not to mention that Curt and I had run into the hotel's executive staff, even though Rachel was adamant about being in the loop on everything.

"I just learned that Flanagan's and Brecker are doing a St. Paddy's Day distributer promo. The prize is a trip to Dublin for their busiest day of the year. I need your help finding a hotel. They're sold out here, like everywhere else, I'm sure. There'll only be ten winners plus guests. I might have you work it."

"Awesome. We can see the Liffey dyed green."

"You'd be working it alone."

Rachel had faith in me to work a meeting abroad by myself?

We'd come a long way since my first meeting in Dublin when she'd only trusted me to dress like a sausage and direct people to the bathroom. I'd managed a meeting alone at Brecker headquarters in Milwaukee, but this would entail working at a hotel four thousand miles away with nobody to fall back on for help. I'd flown solo one day in Paris covering for a planner with food poisoning and Declan, who'd gone MIA. Yet I couldn't decide whether to do a happy dance or throw up.

"If you aren't comfortable working it, I can ask Gretchen."

Gretchen, also a contractor, was Rachel's golden child and a royal bitch. Even worse, she'd slept with Declan.

"I'll do it."

"Perfect. I also have to organize a Flanagan's meeting since they don't have a planner and the president thought I did a *brilliant* job on the October integration meeting here. As if I have time to plan their programs." A contented look spread across her face, usually marred with stress lines creasing her forehead and a vein pulsating in the middle of it.

What was up?

"After New Year's, you could come into the office a few days a week to help out."

"That'd be great."

"I'll have you start on the St. Paddy's Day program later this morning."

"Perfect. I'll be at the desk when you're ready." I headed toward the door.

"Oh, and I slept with Gerry Coffey."

I spun around, wide-eyed. "What?"

She relaxed back in her chair with a dreamy expression, peering out the gold-draped windows at the misty view of a weathered brick building across the alley. "Last night when I left you guys at the market, I went to check out the pub's private room for future events." Her gaze darted to me. "You know we're not related to him. Just share an ancestor's surname."

"Yeah, I know."

My shocked expression wasn't over her having sex with a possible Coffey family member ten times removed. Rachel didn't do one-night stands. And she hadn't had a steady boyfriend since Simon dumped her four years ago when she'd called him bitching about her job while he celebrated his birthday alone at a restaurant.

I headed toward her, lowering my voice. "You did it in their private dining room?"

"No, at his place. He got someone to cover for him. I

just got back an hour ago." She popped the top on another energy drink. "He's so witty, and cute, and..." She sighed. "That Irish accent..."

She recounted the hot and steamy details of them having sex in every room of Gerry's five-room town house. I shot an occasional nervous glance over my shoulder, making sure no attendees were walking in on us. Rachel didn't appear concerned, off in Gerry-land.

I left the office in a sweat over Rachel's sexcapades and keeping my relationship with Declan a secret from her. She'd just placed all of this trust in me to work a meeting alone and confided in me about Gerry Coffey, and I hadn't returned the trust. I planned to tell her about Declan and me at the end of this trip after we proved we could maintain a professional relationship. If she knew about us, she'd be on the lookout for signs of inappropriate behavior.

Yet not confiding in her wasn't exactly appropriate behavior for a sister, and a friend.

Our group's only planned event was a three-hour breakfast daily in the hotel's pub, which opened to the public at noon. A time for winners to share their Dublin experiences and for us to make sure everyone was alive and not incarcerated. Like Curt and Derik. I sat outside the pub at our hospitality desk—draped in a red Brecker-logoed linen—typing on my laptop. Declan strolled out from working breakfast, looking insanely hot in his black suit and white buttoned shirt. Knowing that his oxford was a wrinkled mess except for the ironed front made me smile.

We shared a loathing for ironing.

Declan flashed me a sexy little smile, then peered past me at Finn O'Brien heading toward us, dressed in a navy wool jacket and blue-and-tan plaid scarf.

"Well, that's interesting, isn't it now?" Declan said.

"Omigod," I muttered. "Bernice and Gracie must have mentioned our hotel when they bought wine at his food stand."

I popped up from my chair. The chef smiled at me and nodded hello to Declan. Declan returned his nod, not his smile.

"Thought I'd stop in to firm up tonight. I also wanted to show you this." He laid that morning's newspaper on the table, a spread on last night's Christmas market.

My teeth clamped down on my lower lip, gaze narrowed on a pic of Finn kissing my hand. I looked surprised and like a total dork in that Santa stocking cap.

"Jaysus," Declan muttered, peering over my shoulder.

"Sorry." Finn shrugged with embarrassment. "My mom organizes the charity auction."

Panic zipped through me. "Will she be there tonight with a photographer?" I didn't want photographic evidence of me setting his restaurant's kitchen on fire.

Finn laughed. "No worries. She has other obligations tonight. You have my card with the address. Call in about four. I also wanted to make sure you don't have any allergies or dietary restrictions."

I'd never eaten goose, but I wasn't allergic to other poultry. I shook my head.

Bernice and Gracie walked toward us, wearing clean clothes and big smiles. Brightly patterned leggings broke up the monotony of Gracie's turquoise top and tennies. Bernice had on a purple velour jogging suit and pink tennies.

"Well, hello there. Here to cook Caity breakfast?" Bernice wiggled her brows suggestively.

As if Finn and I had spent the night together.

A low growl vibrated at the back of Declan's throat.

Finn flashed the women his signature smile. "No, just firming up details for tonight."

"Can we come watch and pick up some cooking tips?" Gracie asked.

Declan arched a curious brow. "Yes, can we?"

Finn shrugged. "Sure. The more the merrier."

Gracie gave him a playful swat. "The merrier. Aren't you just in the holiday spirit?"

"Don't worry—you can still dine at a table for two." Bernice gave me a wink.

Declan managed a strained smile.

Finn gestured to our table linen. "Work for Brecker, do ya?"

"I'm a contractor. My sister, Rachel, works for them."

"I was wondering about your beer garments last night. Thought it was a giveaway at the market."

"Just to this trip's winners. But I have extras." I fished a Brecker scarf out from the box under the table and handed it to him.

He probably wore Hugo Boss, but he gave me a

gracious smile. "Thanks. See you tonight." He headed toward the lobby, stopping to chat with Rachel.

A sense of relief washed over me. Finn knowing I worked with Brecker would make a conversation about his restaurants carrying the beer easier. One less thing to worry about tonight. The relief was fleeting since I had plenty of other things to agonize over.

"Feckin' wanker," Declan muttered, marching into breakfast.

Bernice and Gracie were admiring Finn's butt from afar.

Nice. But not nearly as good as Declan's in a pair of jeans.

"Declan mentioned that you traced your Irish ancestry," Bernice said. "We're wondering if you might be able to help us trace our McKinneys in Scotland. Would be nice to have someone to visit when we go there next year."

"I've only done a bit of research in Ireland. My trial Ancestry.com subscription expired."

"We'd compensate you of course. And could help you win a TV, iPad, lifetime supply of fish food, all kinds of stuff."

"How about a car?" My red sports car had been repoed two months ago, and I was still driving my uncle's truck that reeked like wet dog, tobacco, and manure.

"If not a car, at least enough stuff you could sell to buy one," Bernice said.

I smiled. "You've got a deal."

"Great," Gracie said. "We better go eat. Need some strong tea. Was a long night."

Rachel approached. I snatched the newspaper off the table, unsure how she'd feel about my picture.

She gestured to the paper. "I already saw it online. Got a call from Flanagan's CEO, who recognized you from the October meeting. He's ecstatic you were wearing Flanagan's and Brecker's logos while blocking the Guinness banner."

"I was thinking, you should do this thing tonight," I said. "You're the one with all the copper pots and pans hanging over a huge island in your kitchen."

"Because I'd like to cook *someday* when I have time. You're the one in the photo, who tied Flanagan's name to this event. You can't back out. It's a great opportunity for you to get in good with them since you're helping me plan their meeting. And Tom Reynolds is going to be thrilled."

So if I didn't do this, both CEOs would be ticked, and Rachel would take me off planning Flanagan's meeting and spending St. Paddy's Day in Dublin?

"If you secure O'Brien's business, we'll both get a bonus."

Hmm… That made the possibility of torching Finn's kitchen a little more bearable.

Rachel looked baffled. "Why are you so against doing dinner with a hot Irish guy?"

"I'm not. I'll do it."

Rachel had been sympathetic about Andy and hadn't said *I told you so*, but she'd definitely say she'd warned me about Declan.

It would only be a *warning* if things with Declan turned out badly. Did I expect them to?

Rachel headed back to the office.

I plucked the memory card from the company's camera and stuck it in my laptop. I'd taken over a thousand shots to make sure I had at least a couple hundred good ones. I needed an enlarged view to weed out the bad ones. No icon popped up on the screen, asking if I wanted to download new pictures. I reinserted the card. The computer recognized the memory card but still no pics. Had none of the photos saved to the card? I stuck the card in the camera. Nothing. They were just there yesterday. Was it a bad card?

Omigod. I'd lost five days of attendee shots.

Rachel would freak.

My photographer position was my biggest responsibility this program. Rachel would lose faith in my abilities to work a meeting alone. Thankfully, she'd only reviewed the pictures from the welcome reception. The ones that would be the most difficult to reshoot!

I tested a new memory card, taking a shot of the Guinness sign at the pub's entrance. It loaded on my laptop, no problem. I tossed the other card on the table. I flew into the pub, frantically snapping shots of a dozen attendees enjoying a full Irish breakfast. Gracie slipped an arm around Declan's waist, snuggling against him, smiling wide for the camera. I followed a man and his son out to the lobby and had them pose by the Christmas tree. Derik and Curt shuffled out of the elevator, their bloodshot eyes matching their red Brecker T-shirts.

"It's not closed yet, is it?" Derik asked.

"Nope, come on." I directed them into the pub and straight to the bar. No banquet staff around, so I slipped behind the dark paneled counter and grabbed two beers from a fridge. Brecker had special ordered and prepaid all the beer. I opened the bottles and handed them to Curt and Derik. "Say *sláinte*."

Curt's forehead wrinkled in confusion. "Thought you told us to take it easy on drinking?"

"I was kidding. You're here to have a good time."

Even deeper wrinkles creased Curt's forehead. "And you want to have a good time with us?"

"Yep. Now drink."

A smile slithered across his unshaven face. "Cool..."

They clinked their beer bottles together, and I snapped a pic. I took shots from various angles to give the appearance of different pubs—one with the McGregor surname mirror in the background, another with the stained-glass trim running over the top of the bar. I had them finger-comb their greasy hair for one and had Curt slap the beer label in his jeans pocket on his forehead for another. I tolerated their arms around my shoulders for a selfie. Declan flashed me a curious look as he walked out.

"Eat a quick breakfast, and we'll head to the temple bar area," I said.

They slammed their beers.

Curt belched. "Okay, ready."

"Eat something. We have a lot of pictures to take."

Heart racing, I flew out of breakfast to run up to my room and grab my jacket. Bernice and Gracie could meet me at the Christmas market for pics and—

"These snaps are brilliant," Declan said, seated at my laptop.

What snaps?

I bolted over to my computer displaying all the attendee pictures I'd taken. I about collapsed with relief.

I lived to work another day.

"You have a knack for capturing candid shots. People are comfortable around you." Declan looked seriously impressed by my photographer skills.

I nodded. "Thanks. Since you have the memory card in there, can you save them onto my computer?"

I had no clue why the photos wouldn't download before, but no way was I losing them again. I wouldn't have the opportunity to take more. Everyone was on their own tonight, and we'd decided against departure shots since most people were low maintenance on early flights.

"You should think about giving photography a go."

I nodded faintly, refusing to admit my panic attack over the missing pictures. Let Declan be impressed. He didn't need to know every time he came to my rescue on a daily basis without even trying.

CHAPTER FOUR

I squeezed the baster with too much force, causing hot goose fat to spray off the bird, spitting me in the forehead, Finn O'Brien in the face.

I gasped in horror. "Sorry."

"No worries." The chef's usual charismatic smile was a bit lacking in charisma. He slipped the kitchen utensil from my hand and focused on basting, absently wiping his face with a towel.

I fought the urge to pluck several drops of fat from his unshaven chin, not wanting to touch Finn in public when touching Declan was off limits. He, Rachel, Gracie, and Bernice sat lined up in front of the shiny stainless-steel counter in the test kitchen where O'Brien's restaurant held cooking classes and demonstrations.

Rachel snapped a pic of me finger-combing goose fat from my bangs. I'd informed her that as head photographer I had to approve all shots used for promotional purposes.

I wiped the grease from my forehead with the red

ruffled bottom of my fancy apron, a souvenir from Finn. I hadn't put on an apron since I was seven. When helping Grandma bake, I'd worn her purple apron, and Rachel, her yellow sunflower one.

Finn had prepped the goose prior to my arrival, so I hadn't had to dig out the slimy giblets or whatever else might have made me nauseous. It was a small goose, able to feed six people, and only took two hours to cook unstuffed. In the meantime, we made dressing with celery, onions, spices, and goose fat droppings. A good thing this bird had a lot of fat to spare since it was also used to roast the potatoes. A bigger concern than wearing the goose fat on my face was wearing it on my butt for a month.

Except for the fact I hadn't had the opportunity to bring up Brecker beer and secure a bonus, the evening was going much better than I'd anticipated. Finn was doing most of the cooking. I was stirring sauces and measuring ingredients from unmarked containers to retain the chef's secret recipe. I was keeping my distance from sharp knives and flammable materials. Who'd have thought I could cause harm with a baster?

I stirred the brownish-colored gravy with a spicy, vaguely familiar scent... The timer buzzed, and Finn slid the roasting pan from the oven. He sliced through the bird's crispy skin.

My stomach growled. "I'll have white meat, please."

"It's all dark."

"Oh, that's right. I'll take a leg." I used to eat chicken drumsticks when I was a kid.

Finn laughed, sliding a slice of breast meat on my plate. "You have a brilliant sense of humor."

Asking for a leg was obviously a faux pas.

He drizzled gravy over the meat and added sides to our plates. I snapped a pic of the culinary masterpiece, pride welling up inside me. Even though I'd contributed little to the preparation, I'd made it through three hours of cooking, and the only snafu was basting us with goose fat.

I glanced over at Declan, who gave me a thumbs-up.

I cut off a small piece of meat and took a bite.

A horrible taste filled my mouth.

Curry!

A gag reflex prevented me from swallowing the foul taste. Afraid I might projectile vomit goose curry all over Finn, I covered my mouth with my apron and spit it out. I pretended to cough.

"She's choking!" Bernice yelled.

Everyone sprang from their chairs.

In one swift movement, Finn was behind me, wrapping his arms around my middle. He grasped one fist with the other, pressed in below my rib cage, and heaved his hands in an upward motion. I *was* going to vomit. Another big heave, and I waved frantically for him to stop. He lowered his hands and stepped back, wide-eyed and panicked.

Gracie snapped a lovely pic of me still holding my goose-curry-filled apron to my chest. "You saved her life."

"Sorry...went down...wrong way," I sputtered. I chugged my glass of red wine to wash away the horrid taste.

"I caught the entire thing on video if you want to use it to train your staff," Bernice said proudly.

I shot her a mortified look.

Apron still clutched against my chest, Declan drew me into an embrace. He smoothed a hand over my hair, kissing my forehead. "Feckin' A. You scared the shite out of me."

I nestled my head against his chest, comforted by his arms and woodsy cologne. Sensing Rachel glaring at our public display of affection, I stepped back from Declan, avoiding her gaze. Finn was too busy slamming wine from the bottle to notice.

"Um, I'm going to clean off my apron." I fled the kitchen, Rachel hot on my heels.

"I knew this was going to happen," she said as we flew into the bathroom.

"I'm sorry, but you *knew* that I'm a disaster in the kitchen."

"That's not what I'm talking about. I'm talking about Declan. Besides, you spit it out because you didn't like it."

"Yeah, well, everyone else thinks I was choking."

Unless Finn reviewed Bernice's video and realized I hadn't been. I had to delete the evidence from her phone. I needed that bonus. Finn's reaction could go either way. He might carry Brecker because he wouldn't want it getting around that I'd choked on his award-winning goose curry. Or he'd be so traumatized from saving my life that he wouldn't want the beer as a reminder every time he poured a pint of it.

Rachel glared at me, hands on hips. "Didn't I warn you about him?"

"Just because Gretchen thinks he's a player—"

"And dozens of other women. Caity, have more respect for yourself. What makes you think you're any different than all the other girls he's slept with?"

"Because *I* haven't slept with him, and he told me about Shauna's death..."

Rachel's head snapped back in surprise. "Who's Shauna?"

I'd just broken my promise to Declan not to mention Shauna to anyone.

I shrugged. "Someone he was...close to."

"When did she die?"

"Three years ago. He confided in *me* about her when he hasn't talked to anyone else. You can't say a word."

"I won't." Rachel shook her head. "I feel so awful for..." She trailed off, peering over my shoulder.

I turned to find Declan standing in the doorway. My hands dropped to my sides, releasing the apron, remnants of goose curry tumbling to the floor.

How long had he been standing there?

Declan's gaze narrowed. "Was just seeing if you're okay."

Was his concerned expression over me choking or blabbing about Shauna? A sick feeling tossed my stomach, and it wasn't from the lingering taste of curry in my mouth.

"She's doing great." Rachel's sympathetic expression was directed more at Declan than me. "How are *you*?"

I shot her a warning look. *Way to be discreet.*

"I mean, that was pretty traumatic for us also," Rachel said.

"I'm grand." He looked baffled by her concern. "Right, then. I'll wait out here."

He left, and my gaze darted to Rachel. "Gee, that wasn't the least bit suspicious."

"Well, excuse me, but I'm still processing what you just told me and what you *hadn't* told me."

After I told you about Gerry Coffey.

For once, her disappointed expression wasn't over me screwing up my job. She marched out.

Wait a sec. Rachel cared more about the fact that I hadn't confided in her about Declan and me than she had about me likely messing up Brecker's shot with O'Brien's restaurants and our bonuses? This helped lessen the blow that I'd just caused our relationship to take a step backward. And Declan had likely heard me blab about Shauna and would never confide in me again.

Hopefully, I hadn't just lost the two people closest to me.

Thanks to that wretched bird!

CHAPTER FIVE

The festive lights blanketing the brick department stores on Grafton Street did little to perk me up. Neither did the leprechaun wearing a Santa hat and singing carols. I was proud of myself for finding the sweater shop where I'd bought my favorite blue mohair scarf last trip. However, with no money for retail therapy, I decided on comfort food. I popped into a busy coffee shop for some hot chocolate and a scone. I unzipped my purse, and my nose crinkled from the stench of curry pouring out. Not wanting Finn to think I was unappreciative, I'd kept my souvenir apron. The smell clung to my designer handbag, a yellowish smear staining the black lining. I'd just paid off the insanely expensive purse.

I whipped the balled-up cloth into the garbage can.

I pulled out my phone to check messages and realized it was still turned off. After leaving the restaurant, I'd needed a few moments of silence to recover and had forgotten to turn it back on. Rachel had left seven messages merely requesting I call her. Her tone grew a bit angrier with each one. Had the realization just settled in that I'd likely lost O'Brien's business, or was she still upset about Declan and me?

Speaking of which, I had zero messages from Declan.

Not a good sign.

I texted Rachel that I was on my way back.

She asked me to meet her in the office.

I opted to wait in the coffee shop's long line rather than racing back to the hotel to face Rachel and the possible end of our reestablished friendship.

Speaking of friendship, my ex-best friend Ashley and I hadn't spoken in over a year. She'd tried to do an intervention, warning me that Andy was an arrogant, controlling ass. I'd insisted she was merely jealous that I was dating a gorgeous lawyer. My stomach tossed at the thought of choosing that bastard over my best friend.

It tossed again when an e-mail popped up from my client Heather informing me that the February meeting in Venice was canceled. Would I still get paid? I couldn't recall the contract's extensive provisions. I shot Heather an e-mail tactfully asking *when*, not *if*, I would receive my cancellation fee. Besides the possible loss of income, no romantic gondola ride with Declan. If I wasn't meeting Rachel, I'd be in a pub slamming pints rather than sipping hot chocolate!

A half hour later, I headed with a sense of dread down the hotel's hallway toward our office, reminded of a meeting when I had been preparing to confront

Rachel after a big blowup. That argument had ultimately led to mending our strained relationship, caused by Rachel being a workaholic and Andy manipulating me into distancing myself from family and friends.

Maybe my talk with Rachel wouldn't go too badly. Maybe she wasn't going to tell me she'd never hire Declan and me together on a program again or that we were back to being merely sisters rather than friends. Maybe she wanted to tell me I'd screwed up the hotel research I'd been doing for the St. Paddy's Day trip, an excuse to fire me...

I entered the office, where Rachel paced with a nearly empty glass of wine. Exactly how I'd found her the last time.

I took a deep breath. "I'm sorry I didn't tell you—"

"Dad slipped on a patch of ice, shoveling the driveway. Threw out his back and broke his arm. Mom's freaking out about taking care of him, Christmas, having to cancel the party... Pretty much everything."

"Omigod. Is he okay? Is Aunt Teri helping out?"

"She has the flu, and Dottie isn't back yet from Florida."

"She can't cancel the party. It's a tradition. It means a lot to her." I heaved a disappointed sigh. "We'll have to save Killybog for spring after all."

"I already checked, and flights are packed because of Christmas. I could only get one of our tickets changed, and even that was an insane price. So I'll go home and help Mom. I had the rental car changed to your name."

My heart raced. Last trip, I'd almost been hit by a bus, looking the wrong way while *walking* across the street. I couldn't *drive* in Ireland!

Relax. Don't freak out.

"Does Mom know I can't make it home early?"

"Yeah. You staying here by yourself gave her one more thing to worry about. But you planned the trip to Grandma's homeland and made contact with Sadie Collentine. You need to meet her. Need to find answers about Grandma's past."

"But this is supposed to be *our* journey."

Researching Grandma had helped Rachel and me reconnect. After my Declan secret, we really needed sister bonding time in Killybog so I could do some damage control.

"We'll go in the spring like we originally planned." Rachel held her head high, struggling to remain stoic.

"The weather will be better in the spring." I tried to sound reassuring, despite fighting back tears.

"I need to tell you something else." Apprehension filled her voice, and she picked at a manicured nail.

What could be worse than what she'd just told me?

"I was in on the whole Finn cooking thing with Bernice and Gracie."

I knew it!

"They came across an auction promo in the newspaper at breakfast and mentioned wanting to memorialize their sister. I offered to go in on it. Not just for Brecker's sake, for yours."

"For *my* sake?"

"I thought a date with one of Ireland's most eligible

bachelors would give you a morale boost. Of course, I hadn't known about Declan."

"I'm sorry. I planned to tell you when we went to Killybog. I wanted to prove we could still act professional."

Which we'd done until our intimate hug at the restaurant.

Rachel nodded faintly.

Two months ago, I'd have believed her actions were purely motivated by financial and professional gain. I'd be fuming right now. However, after her hurt reaction in the restaurant bathroom, I was touched. Also, a sense of pride welled inside me that Rachel had secretly entrusted me with the responsibility of landing a lucrative piece of business.

And I'd majorly effed up my big break.

I had to contact Finn and land O'Brien's account.

☘ ☘

I was marching out of the office, determined to win Finn's business, when Declan called and asked me to meet him in the lobby. His voice held an ominous tone. I slowed my pace.

He'd heard me blabbing to Rachel.

I would explain that telling Rachel had been an accident. He had to forgive me. Relationships were about forgiveness. Right?

Declan stood in the lobby holding a bouquet of red and white roses. Either he hadn't heard me or he forgave me.

He handed me the flowers.

I smiled wide. "Thanks. They're—"

"From Finn O'Brien." His jaw tightened.

"Oh," I muttered, lowering the bouquet from my nose.

"There's a card."

I opened the small pink envelope and slid out a card containing a two-hundred-euro gift certificate so I could give his restaurant, and goose curry, another chance. My stomach tossed. Apparently, he didn't realize I hadn't choked on his famous recipe. But a two-hundred-euro dinner was insane. Could I exchange it for cash? I should be the one sending him a thank-you gift for supposedly saving my life. He said he hoped to see me next time I was in town to discuss adding Brecker Dark to his menu.

I'd be getting a bonus after all!

If I didn't screw up my second shot with Finn.

"It's a two-hundred-euro gift certificate for O'Brien's restaurant." I left out the part about us seeing each other the next time I was in town.

"Aren't those beautiful," an older woman said, admiring the roses. "He's a keeper." She smiled at Declan, telling her husband how much roses meant to a woman as they walked off.

"Do they?" Declan quirked a curious brow. "Mean a lot to a woman?"

"I'd rather have a guy change the oil in my car than give me flowers." If I had a car. I slipped the gift card into my pocket. I offered the bouquet to another passing couple. "Happy Christmas."

The man gave me a suspicious look. "How much?"

His wife shot him an annoyed glance.

I smiled. "Free. Just spreading holiday cheer."

"Why, thank you, luv." The woman accepted the flowers, and they headed toward the elevator.

I quickly changed the subject from Finn to my dad's accident and Rachel going home rather than to Killybog.

Concern creased Declan's brow, and he took a step toward me. "I hope he's okay. I'll drive you there. No problem a' tall."

A sense of relief washed over me. I wouldn't have to drive, and Declan hadn't heard me in the restaurant bathroom, if he was willing to chauffeur me around Ireland. I had to tell him. I didn't want Rachel to slip up and mention Shauna. It should come from me. However, now wasn't the time, when I was trying to get Declan to confide in me.

He smiled. "I have something that'll make you feel better." Instead of kissing me senseless, he led me over to the towering Christmas tree with twinkling red lights and four green backpacks lying on a red tree skirt. He unzipped one and revealed the contents—colorful pairs of earmuffs, mittens, wool scarves and socks, a McDonald's gift certificate, Christmas candy, and small wrapped gifts. "Happy Christmas. Let's go find some mothers in need."

"Omigod," I muttered. "I could kiss you right now."

With a mischievous smile, he leaned in and whispered in my ear, "Go ahead. Rachel knows about us after our hug in the restaurant." He drew back slightly, a daring glint in his eyes.

Heart racing, I nodded. "Yeah, so we really need to remain professional." This also wasn't the time to mention Rachel's role in setting me up with Finn. "But I'll thank you when we get outside."

Declan's playful expression turned serious. He glanced down at the backpacks, then peered up at me. "I, ah, felt bad in Paris after I told you not to give those women money. I'm sorry I was such an arse. And that I didn't apologize sooner. It's been bugging me."

He'd been a bit judgmental in Paris when I'd given women money after he'd loaned me the cash. However, one filled backpack had to have cost well over a hundred euros.

I spontaneously leaned in and kissed Declan. Not merely a quick peck before anyone saw us, but our lips lingered several moments. I slowly drew back, holding his gaze rather than frantically glancing around for Rachel. He smiled.

"Thank you. This is the sweetest gift ever."

Both his apology and the backpacks.

Last Christmas Andy had given me Tiffany diamond-stud earrings, which I'd recently sold on Craigslist—a popular online advertiser—for three hundred bucks, a fraction of the original cost. His assistant had undoubtedly picked them out. These backpacks made me feel better than diamonds ever could. Declan made me feel better about myself and the future than any man ever had. And the fear of losing him made me realize I was ready to take the next step in our relationship.

I was ready to sleep with Declan.

CHAPTER SIX

The following morning, Gracie and Bernice entered the lobby from the elevator instead of the front door, where Declan and I were dispatching airport departures.

"We won't be needing our shuttle to the airport," Bernice said. "We've decided to stay for New Year's. Our dates went quite well." She winked. "We'll send you links for all our contest forums and copy you on the ones we enter you in. And we bought you a subscription to Ancestry.com so you can research our McKinneys. We'll send you what Scottish family history we have after the holidays."

I smiled. "That wasn't necessary, but thank you." The research site might also help me find more Coffey rellies.

"I don't want to know if you learn anything bad, though," Gracie said.

"Well, depending on *how* bad," Bernice added.

"How bad is bad?" I was curious, since I was debating telling Mom if I confirmed Grandma had been married in Ireland, along with any other family secrets I might uncover.

"Like if you find a murderer in the family," Gracie said.

"But what if he was a famous murderer?" Bernice asked.

Gracie nodded. "I suppose if he was a famous killer like... James Bond famous but certainly not Jack the Ripper famous."

Bernice pondered that a moment. "I think James Bond was English, not Scottish."

"He was an English agent, but in *Skyfall* he went back to his childhood home in the Scottish highlands."

Bernice nodded. "That's right. He was Scottish."

He was *fictional*.

"I'll see what I can do," I said.

Gracie sniffed the air, top lip curling back. "What is that smell? It's not the hotel's cedarwood...it's more spicy..."

Bernice nodded, sniffing with the determination of a hound dog. "Lavender..." Her nose crinkled. "And..."

"Vanilla," I said. "It's my purse. I doused it with the hotel's signature vanilla-lavender-scented spray."

Bernice's nose was still crinkled. "Well, I think they need a new signature scent. No offense, dear, but it's a bit...exotic."

"Because I was trying to cover the smell of goose curry in my purse."

Gracie gasped in horror. "You threw up in your purse?"

"No, it just smells like it. I stuck my apron in there."

"Ah," the ladies said, nodding.

Declan joined in their nodding, having obviously been wondering about my stench.

"Well, it doesn't really smell *that* bad," Gracie said.

Bernice and Declan shook their heads reassuringly, but not real convincingly.

"It had a nice aroma when you were cooking it," Bernice said.

"Which reminds me, could you please delete that video of me choking on the goose?"

"I already did, dear." Bernice gave me a sympathetic pat on the arm.

Phew. One less thing to worry about.

We exchanged good-bye hugs. I almost had to pry Gracie's arms from around Declan. We promised to stay in touch.

Curt and Derik were late for their airport transfer. Our last departure. No way was I delaying our trip to Killybog because those idiots were passed out in a drunken stupor, hopefully in their room and not under a Christmas tree. Curt finally answered his phone, sounding groggy and disoriented.

"Your airport shuttle is leaving." I used my stern motherly tone. "If you aren't down here ASAP, you'll be responsible for the additional hotel nights and rebooking fee, which will be massive. Flights are sold out until after Christmas."

"Shit." The line went dead.

Eight minutes later, they came down reeking of stale smoke and booze, hair uncombed, and clothes spilling out of their half-zipped suitcases.

Curt tripped on his untied shoelaces. He glanced down at his brown tennies, then at the red ones on his buddy's feet. "Dude, we have the wrong shoes on. Your feet are way huge. I can't walk in these."

"You can switch in the car." Declan grabbed Curt's elbow and steered him toward the door, his suitcase wheels bouncing against the marble floor.

Curt almost tripped again walking out the sliding doors.

My mind flashed back to me racing out these same doors and my backless shoe flying off, my phone shooting from my hand as I fell flat on my face in front of Brecker's CEO. He'd disconnected his call to peel me off the ground. I'd been even more mortified when he'd noticed my dancing leprechaun socks from the hotel's gift shop—I'd forgotten to pack socks. Declan had witnessed the entire episode. Within minutes, he'd had me laughing rather than crying, sharing a story about him tripping down the stairs of a moving bus filled with attendees. I smiled at the thought of Declan's tale, rather than cringing at the memory of my embarrassing moment.

We stuck the idiots in a black sedan and slammed the doors.

"If they're denied boarding or miss their flights, it's the airline's issue. I'm not answering my phone."

We returned to the lobby as Rachel exited the elevator pulling two large rolling suitcases. She wore her usual travel attire—black yoga pants, black T-shirt, a black jersey cardigan, and flats. Her hair was pulled back in a clip. She often went casual when traveling. Or did it mean she'd spent another steamy night with Gerry Coffey?

Last night after giving away the backpacks to four

very appreciative and emotional mothers, I'd wanted to pop by Rachel's room and tell her about Declan's thoughtful gift, but it'd been too late. I wanted her to think more highly of him on a personal level and to share the experience with her.

She headed toward us with a somber expression. Declan took her luggage, and we walked in silence out to her waiting vehicle. I struggled to remain strong for both our sakes.

"I'll bring you back a souvenir from Killybog."

"Take lots of pics. I just put in for my spring vacation so I can join you here after the St. Paddy's Day program."

Good to know she still had me working that trip. E-mailing her the encouraging note from Finn, and the impressive candid shots I'd taken, had helped smooth things over between us, professionally anyway.

Rachel eyed Declan. "Take good care of her." Her serious tone bordered on threatening.

Declan nodded. "No worries. Of course, I will."

Her gaze narrowed. "I mean it."

Declan stared her down. "So do I."

"I can take care of myself, thank you," I said jokingly, trying to lighten the mood and prevent a brawl.

Rachel and I hugged. Teary-eyed, she got in the car without looking back. The car disappeared down the street.

Needing a good laugh, I turned to Declan. "Tell me about the claustrophobic client in the elevator."

"I have a better idea."

Declan wrapped his arms around my waist and drew

me snugly against him. He held my gaze until his lips touched mine. I lost myself in the kiss. Besides an overwhelming sense of passion, a sense of freedom and adventure raced through me.

I couldn't wait to learn about Grandma's past.

And to take the next step in my relationship with Declan.

Chapter Seven

"My grandma might have shopped here." I stood in front of a red butcher shop established in 1922. Blue and pink clouds streaked the sky over Killybog's cheerfully painted buildings. "Take one with the sunset in the background."

Declan snapped several shots.

I peered around at the pubs and shops, excitement zipping through me. I'd cruised Killybog's streets via Google Maps dozens of times, but that didn't compare to walking down the same streets Grandma once had.

An old stone church stood at the edge of town.

"That's the church from my grandma's photo." I bolted down the sidewalk toward it. Behind the building, a stone fence surrounded a landscape of weathered Celtic crosses towering over smooth granite headstones. "Too bad it's almost dark, or we could search for Coffey rellies."

A large evergreen wreath hung on the church's

arched wooden door. I stood in front of the entrance, glancing over my shoulder, moving to the right. Having memorized Grandma's picture, I knew precisely the spot where she and her sister had stood in 1935. It sucked that Rachel wasn't here by my side.

After Declan snapped my pic, we tried to enter the church.

"Strange," Declan said. "Don't find churches locked often in Ireland."

I grasped the round iron door knocker and banged it against the wood.

"That's a handle, not a knocker."

Using my shoulder, I pressed all my weight against the door.

"Easy. Someone will think you're trying to break in. Never broken into a church but did get kicked out of one once."

"What did you do to get kicked out of a church?"

A sly smile curled Declan's lips. "Got into a bit of a...disagreement."

"With the priest?"

"No, some wanker who was wrong."

I wasn't sure if me getting kicked out of the Musée d'Orsay in Paris, twice, was worse than being kicked out of a church.

Across the street, a black-and-gold sign on the front of a blue building read *Molloy's*. "Your friend Peter's pub." I ran over and posed for a picture in front of it. "This isn't the pub where you and your friends hijacked the Guinness truck, is it?"

"No, that was Carter's up the road from my parents."

"Let's see if Peter's working so I can thank him for

finding Sadie Collentine. Maybe a Coffey rellie is inside drinking a pint."

Declan opened the red door to Mariah Carey's "All I Want for Christmas Is You." A group of older men dressed in dark suits sitting at the bar gave us curious stares. Strangers probably didn't often pop in to the rural pub. They didn't appear to know Declan. I gave them a little wave, and Declan nodded hello. They nodded back and returned to the horse races on the TV behind the bar.

Silver garland framed the bar's mirror, and a sign read *Full of Holiday Beer*, instead of *Cheer*. The best decoration of all—red bags of cheese-and-onion Taytos. My mouth watered from chip withdrawal.

Declan introduced me to Peter, standing behind the bar. Thirtyish, medium height, lean with short brown hair, his T-shirt read *Lovely Day for a Guinness*.

"Well, it's a Christmas miracle," Peter said. "How are ya, mate?"

Declan shook his friend's hand.

"Thank you so much for hooking me up with my Coffey rellie. I'm meeting her tomorrow." I gestured to the men down the bar. "Any of them related to me, by chance?"

"Any ya fellas related to the Coffeys, are ya?" Peter yelled down the bar.

They all shook their heads.

I hung my green coat over the back of a wooden barstool next to Declan, who was already ordering a whiskey. The pub didn't carry Brecker Dark, so I ordered Flanagan's cider ale and three bags of Taytos. Officially on holiday, I skipped my Brecker Dark sales pitch.

Declan and I clinked glasses. *"Sláinte."*

"Ya still seeing Charlotte?" Declan asked Peter.

He smiled, nodding. "For as long as *she'll* see *me.*"

"Smart man." Declan studied the TV, then slid a bill across the bar toward Peter. "Put a fiver on Mattie's Madness."

"You can bet on horses at a pub?" I asked.

"Betting is Ireland's favorite pastime," Peter said. "Everything from ponies to tractor pulls. Declan ever tell ya about the time we raced tractors and he drove it into a creek?"

I arched a curious brow. "No, he hasn't. Do tell."

Declan rubbed a hand over his mouth, trying to erase his guilty grin. He gestured to the money on the bar. "This race will be done by the time you call in my bet."

Peter waved away his sarcasm and snatched up the phone.

"Have you ever bet on the ponies?" Declan asked.

I shook my head.

He gestured to the TV. "Which one do you fancy?"

I scanned the horses' names listed on the screen and studied the jockeys. "Paddy's Sassy Lassy. Love the name and the jockey's lime green and purple outfit."

Declan laughed. "You're betting on an outfit when the odds are thirty to one?"

I had no clue what that meant. "You asked which I liked."

He peered over at Peter still on with his bookie. "Put another fiver on Paddy's Sassy Lassy."

Peter's gaze narrowed. "Mad, are ya?"

Declan shrugged. "It's what *this* lass wants."

My horse started out way behind, then pulled ahead as they came around a bend. Cheering, I sat on the edge of my stool, leaning forward. Paddy's Sassy Lassy was nose to nose with Declan's horse in the homestretch. My Lassy won by inches.

"Woo-hoo!" I punched a celebratory fist in the air.

Peter placed 130 euros on the bar.

Declan slid the money in front of me. "Fair play to ya. And that's after paying the vig."

"Holy crap. Maybe I can earn side money on horse betting."

The men down the bar raised their pints in congratulations, giving me a thumbs-up and expectant looks. I bought them a round of drinks, then stuck my money in my wallet before I threw it all away on the jockey in the super-cute pink-and-black outfit. I would use it to buy a new purse. Although removing the satin lining had weakened the pungent floral stench, the smell of curry lingered. Maybe merely in my head, but it was there.

Ten minutes later, Declan was placing another bet when a tall dark-haired guy, midthirties, entered the pub. Declan glanced over at him, and panic flashed in his eyes as his body tensed.

"Hello, Declan," the guy said, slowly approaching him.

Declan gave him a sharp nod. "Liam."

Liam gave me a faint smile and nod.

"Heard you'd moved to Cork," Declan said.

"Got married last year and bought a house just up the road."

"Ah, grand. Congratulations."

Liam glanced over at me.

"This is Caity, a coworker," Declan said.

Coworker?

Liam shook my hand. He sat next to Declan, who was staring into his glass. Liam broke the awkward silence by ordering a whiskey.

Declan polished off his drink and ordered a double. "Be right back." He disappeared down a dark hallway. I hoped he was going to the bathroom, not escaping out the back door and ditching me.

Why was Declan avoiding this guy?

Liam took a swig of whiskey.

I took a sip of ale.

"Maybe this wasn't such a grand idea," Liam told Peter, swirling the golden liquid in his glass.

"He'll come around." Peter's tone was more hopeful than confident.

This wasn't an accidental encounter. Had Peter snuck in a call to Liam when phoning in our bets? I slid my gaze to the empty hallway.

Liam raised a curious brow. "A coworker, are ya? I'd heard he's a tour guide now."

"Not really a tour guide." I explained our job, giving it a glamorous slant. I also mentioned we were there thanks to Peter and Declan finding my rellie.

Declan returned. He slammed his whiskey and motioned to Peter for another. "So how are your mum and dad?" he asked Liam.

"Grand. You should call on them."

Declan nodded faintly, focusing on the TV.

"You know, they didn't just lose a daughter—they also lost a son. It was hard on them that ya didn't come around. Hard on us all."

Liam was Shauna's brother?

Declan nodded in understanding. Yet he knocked back his third whiskey in one gulp, then stared into the empty glass.

Liam swirled his whiskey some more and polished it off. He placed money on the bar, picking up our tab. "They're in the same house." He gave Declan a pat on the back. "Take care, mate. Tell your family Happy Christmas."

Declan nodded, still focusing on his glass rather than Liam. "You too."

Liam told me good-bye and walked out.

I let out a whoosh of air, almost expelling my lungs from my chest. I wasn't about to narc on Peter for calling Liam, because it was good for Declan to finally face him—and his past.

However, he'd successfully avoided both.

"Are you okay?" I asked.

"Feckin' brilliant." Declan slid off his barstool. "Let's go."

"Um, I'm not done with my drink."

He polished off my nearly full pint in three gulps.

"You can't drive," I said.

He slipped his car keys from his jeans pocket and dangled them in front of me. "You're right. Drunk-driving laws are fierce now."

I stared at the keys, my heart racing. "*I* can't drive."

Declan driving while over the legal alcohol limit would be safer than me driving sober. However, I didn't want him to risk losing his license. At least his family was at his aunt's in Waterford, so our first introduction wasn't me bringing home their drunken son.

My heart skipped a beat.

We'd be alone at Declan's house.

"It's just up the road. You probably won't encounter another car the entire way."

He'd once mentioned Killybog was almost a half hour from his parents. Far from just up the road. He dropped the keys on the bar in front of me. He shook Peter's hand and left.

I reluctantly grabbed the keys and my coat. I thanked Peter again for his help and headed toward the door, car keys clutched in my hand, a sick feeling in my stomach. Not just because I was about to put our lives in danger, but I had the feeling Declan wasn't going to discuss Liam. It hurt that he didn't care to share his feelings. Visiting Killybog and our families' homeland meant different things for us. Being here should provide him the perfect opportunity to come to grips with his past so that we could have a future. I didn't expect him to spill his guts about Shauna, but if we were going to have a relationship, he at least had to be able to discuss her brother. And introduce me as a *friend* rather than a *coworker*.

Damnit. Declan was usually the responsible one taking control of a situation, making it all better, coming to my rescue.

What if *I* wasn't able to rescue *him*?

CHAPTER
EIGHT

Snow. Darkness. A drunken navigator. Driving on the opposite side of the road. Any other obstacles?

Declan stood leaning against the front of the pub, hands stuffed in his jacket pockets, staring down at the snow-dusted sidewalk. We walked in silence for several blocks to Declan's tiny silver car.

I eyed the vehicle. "It's so small."

"Better to have more room on the road than in the car."

Unless I went *off* the road.

I clicked the doors unlocked. We both grabbed the cold metal door handle. Declan's hand warmed my entire body. The first time he'd touched me since we'd arrived in Killybog. I leaned in to kiss him, to reassure him that everything would be okay. He snapped his hand back, startling me. I was finally emotionally ready to sleep with Declan, and now he wouldn't even kiss me?

"Ah, wrong door." He gestured to the steering wheel on the other side.

"Oh yeah." I went over and slid onto the driver's seat. I searched for the ignition, a bit flustered by Declan backing away from a kiss.

"Take a left," he said.

"Let me turn on the car before you start giving me directions."

He pressed a button by the steering wheel. Nothing. "Clutch in, is it?"

I pushed in the clutch, and the car hummed to life. Crap. I'd been praying it wouldn't start. My repoed sports car had a manual transmission, but I was so nervous I couldn't remember how to drive one. It didn't help that the seat was on the opposite side, requiring me to use my left hand instead of my right to shift. It was like learning to write with the opposite hand. After I turned several switches and knobs, the lights and wipers came on.

"Just remember, your arse is on the line," Declan said.

"Thanks for the reminder."

"No, keep telling yourself that you're sitting on the center, that your arse is on the line. So you'll remember which side of the road to stay on."

Good tip.

My arse is on the line. My arse is on the line...

I backed out and headed down the street, unable to believe I was driving on the opposite side of the road. My confidence diminished when I reached the edge of town and the shoulder disappeared into a farmer's stone fence. No lines marked the narrow road's center or sides. Even though the snow was melting as it hit the pavement, it was hard to judge where I was at on the road until several branches scraped the passenger door. Whatever eighty kilometers converted to in miles was way too fast for the winding road.

A car's approaching headlights caused my grip to tighten on the steering wheel. My first instinct was to squeeze my eyes shut. Instead, I slowed to a crawl, hugging the side of the road, deciding it was better to hit a fence than a car. The car passed, and I heaved a relieved sigh. I rounded a corner and encountered an elderly man in a yellow reflective vest walking a small dog. I gasped, swerving into the other lane. He jumped onto a narrow strip of grass, taking his dog with him. Luckily, no car in the other lane.

Declan appeared unfazed by our near-death experience. Either he was preoccupied replaying his conversation with Liam in his head, the alcohol was kicking in, or this was just your typical Ireland driving experience.

A roundabout appeared out of nowhere. "Omigod. What do I do?" Heart racing, I put a death grip on the steering wheel.

"You're grand. Yield to the right, drive to the left."

Yield, drive, yield, drive...

No cars to the right, I turned left into the roundabout. Three roads exited off of the circle. "Which one do I take?"

"The first."

Having just passed the second, I drove around again. A car zipped into the circle, and I pressed on the brake without downshifting. Our car rocked to a halt. The other car veered off onto the first exit. Taking deep breaths to regulate my short, shallow ones, I waited to regain enough confidence to start the car or for Declan to sober up enough to drive.

Whichever came first.

A car honked and swerved around us.

Declan glared at the passing driver. "Nearly hit ya, he did. Why ya stopping?"

I gave Declan the evil eye, then gave myself a pep talk. A sitting duck in the roundabout, I pushed in the clutch and started the car. I drove around the circle once more, then took the first road out of hell. Driving on the opposite side was turning out to be the easiest part of navigating Ireland's narrow roads.

Twenty minutes later, I was about to ask if we were almost in Northern Ireland, when Declan said, "It's just up the road."

Declan's town lit up the sky in the distance. Thank God. The end was in sight. But rather than a small village illuminating the dark sky, it was Declan's parents' yard, decorated for the holidays.

"It's best to say we're just friends, or my mum will interrogate the bloody hell outta ya."

My gaze darted to Declan. "I thought your family was at your aunt's?"

He raked a hand through his hair. "Oh, ah, yeah, they're not."

"You *lied* to me?"

He peered out the window. "No, not really."

"Not really?"

"They were supposed to go but decided not to."

"When?"

"Few weeks ago."

"I got here a few *days* ago, and you said they were gone."

"Yeah, sorry about that."

So if I hadn't had to drive his ass home, I'd never have known he'd lied. Not to mention, he could have called home to have someone pick us up at the pub!

Fuming, I drove up the candy cane-lined driveway. In the yard, wire sheep guided a red sleigh driven by a blow-up Grinch, his small brown dog, Max, in the passenger seat, with a glowing red nose. Wooden cutouts of Whoville and its residents included Cindy Lou Who and several Minions. Colored lights covered every tree and shrub and framed the windows of the large two-story yellow home. Sturdy cloth antlers jutted from the windows of a small blue car, a red nose wedged in its grill.

Womp. I hit something.

I slammed on the brakes.

Omigod. What had I run into?

Clumps of snow trailed across the hood. A blond girl in a purple jacket and jeans stood in front of us grinning, swiping her mittens together. I'd been so overwhelmed by the lights I hadn't noticed her whipping a snowball at us. I let out a relieved sigh that I hadn't hit their family pet. I recognized Zoe from Facebook. She was twenty-five, a year older than me, four years younger than Declan. She apparently shared her brother's sense of humor. I'd been anxious to meet her, just not under these circumstances.

Declan's mom turned from hanging a wreath on the front door, her curious gaze narrowed on me. I smiled, a nervous feeling in my stomach, even though we weren't revealing our relationship status, which I was starting to question.

I peeled my white-knuckled grip from the steering wheel. I wiggled my fingers, trying to regain the circulation. We stepped from the car, and Zoe ran over and launched herself at Declan, throwing her arms around him, causing him to stumble back against the car.

She waved a hand in front of her crinkled nose. "Stopped for a pint or two, did ya?"

Declan's mom introduced herself as Jane. Her welcoming smile eased the tension in my neck. Declan had her bright-blue eyes, which still held a glint of curiosity.

Before I could introduce myself, Zoe gave me a huge hug. "Caity! I didn't know you were coming."

"You two have met?" his mom asked.

Zoe nodded. "On Facebook."

"I work with Declan." Now *I* was referring to myself as merely a coworker, after Declan had upgraded me to friend status.

"Isn't this snow fab?" Zoe squealed with delight. "Do you get much snow where you live?"

"We had thirty-two inches in three days last year with five- to ten-foot drifts. My dad opened the garage door, and we could only see a few inches of light over the top of the snow drift."

Zoe's eyes widened. "What'd he do?"

"Closed the door."

She laughed. "I'm coming to visit you next year. It'd be lovely to see that much snow. I'd never go inside."

"You'd get sick of it pretty quick."

Zoe shook her head. "I wouldn't. I'm seriously coming for a visit. Never been to the States."

"Leave the poor girl alone," Declan's mom said. "She hasn't even taken her bag from the boot, and you're making plans to pack your own for a visit."

"I see you and Tara Gavigan are still competing." Declan gestured to the lit-up yard.

"Every time I put up a new decoration, that woman puts one up. Trying to outdo me, she is."

"She could never outdo you. Dublin could divert planes here." Declan kissed his mother's cheek, putting a bright smile on her face.

He grabbed his suitcase from the car's *boot*, chatting with Zoe.

Jane studied me with interest, smiling. "This is a nice surprise. I had no idea that Declan was bringing a friend," she mused over this discovery.

"We're coworkers. I'm staying at a B and B. I need to go check in, if someone could please take me."

"You'll do no such thing. You'll be staying here with us."

No way was I staying in a bedroom down the hall from Declan, especially after he'd lied about his parents being gone.

Overhearing his mother's invite, Declan stopped talking and appeared to sober at the thought of me staying there.

"I appreciate it but—"

"No buts." Jane pulled my brown carry-on from the trunk.

"That'd be fab if you stayed." Zoe turned to Declan. "Wouldn't it, now?"

He nodded faintly, an apprehensive look in his eyes. Zoe looped an arm through his, leading him toward the house.

"Which B and B?" his mom asked.

"Cullens."

She waved away my concern. "Claire Cullen would rather be spending her time shopping for Christmas pastries in Dublin than baking scones for guests. Only runs the place because she needs a hobby. She won't mind if you cancel. I'll give her a ring."

"I don't want to impose."

"I won't have you paying for a room when I have a perfectly fine one here for free."

The reservation was under penalty at this point, so Claire Cullen wouldn't care if I canceled. Rachel had it guaranteed to her card. Not having much choice, I hauled my suitcase from the trunk.

"I'm glad you drove," Jane said. "A half-pint and the garda will pull you over. It's hurting the rural pubs. Luckily, Carter's is just a short walk up the road. But I see Declan couldn't wait and had to get an early start. That difficult for him to come home for a visit, is it?" A hurt expression creased her face.

"We stopped at Molloy's in Killybog to thank his friend Peter for locating my relative, and Shauna's brother, Liam, showed up."

"Ah, did he now..." She nodded in understanding, yet looked surprised. Possibly that I knew about Shauna? She let out a deep sigh. "Thanks for minding him."

I was still upset over Liam, and Declan lying about his parents, but my anger diminished. For all the times he'd looked out for me, I owed him one, or rather several dozen.

We stepped inside the house. The scent of freshly baked goods filled my head, and the feeling started returning to my fingers. Red garland wrapped around the stairway banister and framed the doorways off the yellow hallway. The interior was more tastefully decorated than the exterior. I hung my jacket on a hook over several pairs of wellies lined up on a mat. Declan's suitcase sat in the foyer. His and Zoe's voices echoed from a room down the hall.

Declan's mom carried my brown bag, and I schlepped my purple suitcase up the stairs. I balanced the suitcase on each step while Jane pointed out the people in photos lining the wall, including a younger Declan. His eyes were even bluer and his hair lighter, yet it still had that tousled look and natural wave. Next to his photo was a black-and-white antique wedding photo of a couple with their names written in blue ink across the top. *Thomas Flood and Catherine Darcy Flood.*

"That's a neat picture," I said. "Who are they?"

"Not sure, but it's a lovely snap, isn't it?"

It was sad when photos were passed down without noting the people's relationship. The photo of Grandma and her sister was our oldest family photo.

Jane frowned at an empty nail. She glanced down at the foyer, then back at the nail and lowered her voice. "That was Declan and"—she mouthed *Shauna's*— "engagement snap there. He took it down. I haven't put another up, hoping one day he'd want it back there..." She shook her head in defeat.

I stared at the empty nail. Who'd have thought a nail could look so lonely, so sad?

Declan's mom opened the door at the top of the stairs, jarring me from my thoughts. "You'll be here in the green room."

I hauled my suitcase up the rest of the stairs and joined her in the bedroom. Christmas decorations filled sage-colored walls. Green lights twinkled on a small tree in a corner. A snowman and Santa pillow lay against the green-and-red quilt.

"Thank you for bringing Declan home early. The last several years he's merely shown up Christmas day, then jetted off somewhere for work." Her voice cracked, and she paused a moment. "This is a very special Christmas, having him here to decorate the tree and spend time as a family. Especially since Aidan won't be home until Christmas Eve."

"You're welcome, but I didn't really do anything."

"If he wasn't bringing ya here to meet your rellie, he wouldn't have come home this early. So thanks a mil for making my Christmas wish come true." She gave my hand a squeeze. "Could be you're just what he needs to get back in sorts."

Maybe Declan's family was just what *I* needed. Together, could we help Declan put the past behind him?

CHAPTER NINE

I stood in the hallway, eyeing several closed doors, wondering which room was Declan's and if it looked the same as when he was growing up. My childhood room did. Tempted to sneak a peek at his past, but not wanting to get caught snooping, I headed down the stairs. The empty nail on the wall was more haunting than if their engagement picture still hung there. Had it been taken in a photo studio or outdoors next to a field of sheep? Had Declan worn his usual jeans and a wool sweater, or had he spiffed up for the occasion? What had Shauna looked like? If Liam was a good representation of their family genes, she'd been gorgeous. I shoved aside visions of the photo.

At the bottom of the stairs, a large curio cabinet displayed wooden nutcrackers lined up at attention. Nutcrackers creeped me out. Their slanted eyes and brows gave them evil expressions, like they were preparing to stab someone with their spears. One was missing an arm, another a leg, and several most of their paint.

"Welcome to the island of misfit decorations," Zoe said. "When a decoration is damaged or hideously ugly, my mum can't help but feel sorry for the poor yoke and buy it because nobody else will. She thinks everyone deserves a home at Christmas. And she always chooses the most pathetic Charlie Brown tree of the lot." Zoe slid her gaze toward the room down the hall, where everyone had gathered, then back at me. "Can you keep a secret?" she whispered.

I nodded, hoping for a deep, dark secret about Declan.

"We decorated the tree weeks ago, then undecorated it last night so we could do it again with Declan. Mad, hey? But it means a lot to my mum, so we didn't argue. Besides, that means more cookies and mulled wine. A tree-decorating tradition." She hooked her arm through mine and led me to the living room.

Flames danced in a green cast-iron stove tucked into a brick fireplace, emitting a strong earthy scent. The overstuffed red furnishings made me want to curl up on the couch with a glass of wine. Christmas prints hung on the cream-colored walls, including one of a little girl placing a star on top of a tree. Declan once mentioned he was an artist. Had he painted it?

A glass of mulled wine in hand, Declan stood relaxed, chatting with his dad, who was stringing lights on a tall, scrawny evergreen tree in the corner. Open cardboard boxes with ornaments and presents filled its tree skirt. Declan introduced me as Caity, rather than *coworker* Caity.

Colin was a handsome man in his fifties, with graying hair, gentle blue eyes, and a charming smile. Exactly how I pictured Declan in twenty years, except Declan had bluer eyes, currently glassed over from too much alcohol. A contented smile curved his lips and warmed my entire body. I had to let Liam and Declan's lie about his parents go. I couldn't allow it to ruin my trip to Killybog.

Declan handed me a glass of mulled wine, which warmed me even more. I slipped off my green cardigan and draped it over the back of a chair, next to an orange cat. The animal wore a knitted reindeer stocking cap with a pom-pom on the end, its ears sticking through two slits next to the antlers.

Zoe turned on music and sang along to "Mele Kalikimaka." She wrapped silver garland around her neck for a lei and hula danced to the Hawaiian Christmas carol. She swayed her hips against Declan's until he joined in dancing. He appeared so comfortable with his family. Not like it'd been eight months since he'd been home. Was it the whiskey and mulled wine?

"This song was in *National Lampoon's Christmas Vacation*," Zoe said. "Have you seen it?"

"Every year," I said. "It's my favorite."

"It's Declan's fave also."

Declan nodded. "Brilliant movie."

My phone rang. Mom. The call failed. She was probably checking to make sure I was tucked in safely at the B & B. No way was I telling her I was staying with Declan. I hadn't mentioned our relationship for fear she'd slip up and say something to Rachel. I wasn't sure how she'd react to me dating. I hadn't given her the entire scoop on Andy, knowing she'd make it her mission to find me an appropriate young man. The same way she'd been trying to find me an appropriate job since I'd lost mine, sending me applications and submitting my résumé without my knowledge. However, if she wanted input on the holiday party, I couldn't leave her hanging.

I excused myself to step outside to return her call. A set of French doors led into a sunroom with a red-cushioned wicker couch and chairs. A pair of yellow wellies with an orange beak painted on the toes and googly eyes stood by the door. Zoe's, no doubt. I told myself they were ducks and not the rancid bird that had caused my mortifying mishap. I stuffed my feet and pants legs inside them.

I walked outside, the brisk air cooling my wine-flushed cheeks. The front-lawn decorations lit the sky over the backyard. I stepped from the wooden deck, and my feet sank into the cushioned grass. A moo echoed in the distance. A gray cat nosing around a shed spotted me and let out a meek meow.

"What's wrong, baby?" I cooed.

I slowly approached the animal. A vicious bark shattered the silence. The cat's back arched, its fur puffing out. I about peed my pants. The barking continued from behind the shed. The cat shot across the yard toward a field. I raced for the house. I flew through the back door, slamming it shut while glancing over my shoulder for a ferocious dog. Heart pounding, I turned and ran smack into Declan, splaying my hands across his chest, his heart thumping against my palms. Our gazes locked.

Realizing everyone had joined us, Declan stepped back and I lowered my hands.

"I didn't know"—I sucked in a shaky breath—"you have a dog."

"Don't have a dog, merely his bark." Jane glared at her husband. "Colin's alarm on the fuel shed." She gave him a swat to the chest. "Nearly gave the poor girl a heart attack, ya did. You were supposed to adjust the sensors."

"Sorry 'bout that," Colin said. "When you go out to the loo, steer clear of the shed."

They had an outhouse?

"He's only messin' with ya," Declan said.

"Turn that bloody thing off," Jane commanded over the barking.

"Ya won't be saying that once I perfect it and we're making millions selling the yokes." Colin marched outside to deactivate the alarm.

"Worried about theft with the recession and cost of fuel so high," Jane said.

"It doesn't keep the neighborhood *cat* burglars away," I said. "I just gave some cat a heart attack."

"It's motion and time sensored. Only goes off at night if a person approaches it. Used to go off every time a bunny hopped by until the neighbor threatened to take his hurling stick to it. *I'm* going to take one to it. Come inside, luv, and we'll get you some mulled wine and cookies."

I sent a text telling Mom I'd call when I had better cell service. And when my voice wasn't trembling with fear. I returned to the living room and gulped down a mulled wine. The orange cat was curled up on my sweater, sound asleep, undisturbed by the alarm.

"I can't believe your cat allows you to dress him up."

Zoe rolled her eyes. "Quigley is totally mad. He growls if we try to take the cap off. My granny, auntie, and I make them to sell at craft markets. It's crazy what people spend on their pets. The extra quid is brill until I graduate in May and open my own decorating shop."

"My mom once tried to put an elf hat on our cat Izzy and ended up in the emergency room with a wicked bite Christmas Eve."

"Zoe ended up in the A and E Christmas Eve after cutting the roof of her mouth on a cookie," Declan said.

"Wasn't my fault. You could stab someone with Auntie Fiona's candy cane sugar cookies. Of course, Mum didn't tell her that her cookie put me in the A and E and made up some mad story that I had a paper cut in my mouth. I'd have to be totally daft to do such a thing."

"I wouldn't be ripping on Auntie Fiona's baking." Declan smirked.

"What? I'm a brilliant baker."

"Like the time you couldn't get gingerbread cookie dough rolled out, so you stuck it in a loaf pan, thinking you'd make ginger *bread*?"

I smiled. "I can totally relate." I shared my broiled banana bread story.

We all laughed.

Thankfully, Declan didn't bring up my goose curry incident.

"Did Declan ever mention that he fancies dolls?"

Declan rolled his eyes. "Doesn't this story ever get old?"

Zoe grinned. "Nope. One Christmas he got up early and unwrapped every bloody present under the tree, including mine. Took a fancy to my Barbie doll and wouldn't give her up. I cried for two days until the stores reopened and Santy brought me another."

Declan shrugged, palms up. "I was eight. I thought she was hot."

I tried to convince myself that Declan hadn't wanted me to meet his family for fear of all the embarrassing stories they'd disclose.

His dad finished weighting down the scrawny tree branches with lights, and we began decorating. Zoe held up a glass ball ornament. Santa had an orange suit, Rudolph a pink nose. "Declan painted these one year for our mum and dad. He's quite talented—just a wee color blind."

"I was avant-garde," he said. "Like Picasso."

He'd stopped painting after his muse, Shauna, died. I'd discovered that the hard way in Paris, sticking my foot in my mouth as usual. I certainly wasn't going to ask if he'd done the painting on the wall.

After we finished decorating, I helped Zoe stack empty ornament boxes by the stairs to be carried up to storage. Something slid around inside one. I removed a snowman ornament.

"We missed one," I said.

Zoe snatched the ornament from my hand, her gaze darting to her parents and Declan chatting in the living room. She tossed it back in the box. "We don't put that one up. It's dated the year...she died."

It was dated three years ago, so I knew who *she* was.

Apparently saying Shauna's name was taboo.

Declan's family wasn't going to give me insight into Shauna, or help him heal, if they didn't even dare utter her name out loud. Declan wasn't the only one who needed to heal.

I glanced up at the empty nail on the wall. A sadness hung over the house that all the festive Christmas lights and cheery decorations couldn't hide.

Supposedly, a picture was worth a thousand words, yet so was the absence of one.

CHAPTER TEN

Peering out the car window at Killybog's colorful buildings, I drummed my fingers against the crinkly plastic wrap containing the gingerbread house. We were getting closer to Sadie Collentine's and to uncovering Grandma's past.

Declan stifled a yawn, attempting to shake the sleep from his head. As we drove past Molloy's, he glanced over at me with bloodshot eyes. "Sorry about drinking so much at the pub. But driving is another first for ya."

"It also could have been my first accident."

"Speaking of accidents, me driving the tractor into the creek was Peter's fault. We were at his uncle's. I had no idea there was a creek. At least it wasn't a Deere."

I smiled despite Declan avoiding the topic of getting drunk because of Liam.

Sadie's yellow ivy-covered bungalow sat just outside of town. Puffs of smoke rose from a stone chimney, filling the air with the earthy scent of peat. The house's green wooden door swung open and out stepped a petite elderly lady and man. She wore a dark-green wool coat, and a fancy black hat with feathers sat atop her tightly curled gray hair. A dark suit swallowed the man's thin frame. They looked like they were off to church. Had we miscommunicated on our meet time? I should have called and reconfirmed our visit.

We returned their enthusiastic waves. Declan took the platter of cookies his mom had made, while I carried the gingerbread house and the wrapped photo and letters.

Sadie's blue eyes sparkled, and she wore a welcoming smile. "It's grand to finally meet ya." She gestured to the gingerbread house. "Oh my, that's simply lovely."

"Lovely." The man nodded in agreement, straightening his red bow tie.

"And so is that." She gestured to the Coffey pin on my purse strap. I wore the pin with the hope that random Coffeys might approach me and inquire about my family history.

We stepped into the foyer, which was filled with the aroma of pumpkin spice. We set the cookies and presents next to a stack of holly wreaths on a credenza.

Sadie folded me into a warm embrace, her hat's feathers tickling my nose. She placed a hand on the gentleman's arm next to her. "This is me cousin Seamus. Your grandmum's sister Ellen's son."

Mom's middle name was Ellen. She hadn't known she was named after her aunt until I found the family in the 1911 census. Sadie and Seamus were Mom's first cousins, yet at least twenty years older than her.

Grandma had been in her early forties when she'd had Mom, now fifty-eight.

The man smiled wide. "Seamus. Like the famous sheep."

His only sheeplike feature was the white tufts of hair on the sides of his otherwise bald head. Thick black-framed glasses weighed heavy on his hollow cheeks.

Sadie smiled at Declan. "I don't think you can be Rachel, now can ya, lad?"

I explained the reason for Rachel's absence.

"Oh my, that's too bad. Hope your father's on the mend."

Seamus shook his head. "Too bad."

"I know you just arrived, but we were thinking if it's all right, it might be best to go straight out before you get your coats off. Seamus just had cataract surgery, so his sight isn't the best, and I'm not driving right now due to...a wee incident." The two of them exchanged nervous glances. "'Twasn't me fault."

I'd be the last person to judge anyone for having an accident on these roads.

"Anyway, we thought this would be a lovely way for you to meet your rellies."

"That'd be great. Where are we going?"

"The cemetery." She grabbed a stack of holly wreaths off the credenza. "Such a lovely day for a cemetery visit, it is. Best to get the wreaths placed before the winds pick up, as they're expected to be fierce."

I shot Declan a discreet glance, which he avoided. A meltdown in a Paris cemetery had led him to confide in me about Shauna's death. This would hit much closer to home than some random Paris cemetery.

We piled into the small car. A few miles up the road, we encountered an abandoned medieval church with an uneven landscape of gravestones and weathered Celtic crosses covered in ivy and moss. I stepped from the car, and a brisk wind cut through me. I nestled into the blue mohair scarf wrapped around my neck. Declan's gaze narrowed on the cemetery.

Please go in. Face your demons.

"I'm gonna wait here," Declan said. "Need to ring a client."

My telepathic abilities were obviously on the fritz.

Declan pulled out his phone to place his fictitious call.

I tried to hide my disappointment. After all, this cemetery visit was about meeting my dead rellies.

Sadie, Seamus, and I passed by the old church. I stopped and peeked through a narrow, arched window. Between the wavy distorted glass and dark interior, I could vaguely make out green foliage growing up a wall. I joined my rellies in the cemetery. Evergreen wreaths, small mangers, Santa figurines, and miniature Christmas trees decorated both older and newer graves. More recent graves lined the front of the cemetery, providing easy access, while older ones stood farther back on uneven ground overgrown with grass and ivy.

"Nice to see people still respect some traditions, placing wreaths on graves at Christmas," Sadie said. "Such a shame that much of society has moved away from holding a proper Irish wake. Don't see as many as you used to, and certainly not as grand as they once were."

Seamus shook his head in disgust. "Won't be putting me body in the ground without a proper wake."

Sadie stopped in front of a large tombstone engraved with a Celtic cross and introduced me to her sister Catherine Ryan, who'd written Grandma about her sister's death. "It's a shame we didn't know you last year before Catherine passed. Was the grandest wake Westmeath had ever seen."

"Simply grand." Seamus smiled, a reminiscent glint in his gray eyes.

"Don't know how I'll outdo it. But I will." Sadie gave me a wink. She gestured to the wreaths in her cousin's stack. "I think you have the artificial one." She peered over at me. "Catherine was allergic to spruce." She secured a green plastic wreath on a stake in the ground so it didn't fly away.

"Can you take our picture by the tombstone?" I asked Seamus. "Might sound strange, but I want to make a family scrapbook."

"Not odd at all, luv," Sadie said. "Our cousin has an album filled with selfies of her and rellies in their coffins. 'Tis a bit disrespectful."

It took me a few moments to recover from that vision and to teach Seamus how to operate my phone's camera feature. After he snapped several pics, I snapped one of them, just in case.

At the next grave, they slowly shook their heads.

"Paddy Smyth was me sister Julia's husband," Sadie said. "What a funeral that was, never seen the likes of it before and hope we never do again. Julia was so distraught she threw herself on the casket. Wouldn't have been so bad if it hadn't already been lowered into the ground. Cracked two of her ribs and the top of the casket. Just a wee crack, but she demanded that Martin Shea, who'd sold her the casket and attended the burial, replace the casket straight away. That her Paddy wasn't being buried in no dodgy casket. Martin insisted she was mad. She told everyone about the incident, and a year later he went out of business."

I came from a very assertive line of women.

"I can't imagine loving someone so much I'd throw myself against his casket in the ground," I said. Maybe that was how I should evaluate my relationships. *Do I love this guy enough to throw myself into his grave?*

"If you do, don't be wearing no dress," Sadie said.

"Or at least have on a proper pair of knickers." Seamus rolled his eyes. "Aye, what a sight that was."

Sadie took a pic of Seamus and me next to the tombstone. We continued on to a grave for Jimmy and Theresa Lynch, née Coffey, Grandma's sister. The epitaph read *Last Call*. Sadie removed a silver flask from her purse and poured a golden-colored liquid over the graves. Whiskey, I assumed.

"Me parents were publicans. Me nephew Riley runs it now. Oh, Mum, can you believe this is Bridget's granddaughter from the States?" Sadie handed me a wreath. "You place it on the grave. She'd like that."

I knelt down and secured the wreath on the stake, emotion weighing heavy on my chest. How sad that Grandma had never visited her sister's grave or attended her funeral. I couldn't imagine not being able to say good-bye to Rachel. "Thank you so much for writing my grandma. She kept your letters." I swallowed the hard lump in my throat, my eyes glassing over with tears. "If it wasn't for those letters, I wouldn't be here right now. She loved you dearly."

Sadie gave my shoulder a comforting squeeze. "She knows, luv."

Three ivy-covered tombstones, surrounded by a leaning wrought iron fence, stood on raised ground, back from our family graves. "Are those Coffeys?"

"Aye," Seamus said. "Don't recall how they were related, going back a ways."

"Watch your footing," Sadie said as I traipsed through the tall grass toward the graves. "Be careful not to trip on a toppled-over tombstone or step in a sinkhole."

What a hole sunk *to*, I didn't care to know.

I touched my foot cautiously on the ground before placing my weight on it. Seamus followed me, but Sadie remained behind in her black heels. Two of the graves were too weathered to read, but a lead-engraved one had survived the harsh Irish weather. I entered the fenced-in area and stripped the ivy from the front of the stone for better viewing. It noted that Christopher Coffey, who died in 1834, played an integral role in the Rebellion of 1798.

A sense of pride welled up inside me. "What role did he play?"

Seamus enthusiastically recounted a story about how Christopher Coffey had dodged a major ambush, saving the lives of his troops. They went on to play a vital role in winning several future battles.

"Now, we aren't sure about the authenticity of that story," Sadie called out. "You know how family lore is— that might be a wee bit of an embellishment."

No, I didn't know how family lore was. I had no ancestor stories to pass down to my children. A sad feeling crept over me. What happened when the lead-engraved tombstone became too weathered to read, like the others? Would they all crumble into the earth and these ancestors be forgotten? I felt a sense of duty to document Sadie's and Seamus's stories for past generations' sakes, and future ones. Grandma certainly never realized that her past would have such a strong impact on my life. She'd made me more courageous, adventurous, and in tune with the importance of family.

What impact would *my* life have on future generations?

CHAPTER ELEVEN

On the way back to Sadie's, we made a detour to visit Grandma's childhood home. I hadn't even considered that her home might still be standing. However, Ireland respected old buildings. Abandoned stone structures dotted the countryside, blending in with the landscape until they naturally returned to the earth once again.

"That's it." Sadie pointed to the side of a stone cottage next to the road as we zipped along.

A grass strip growing up the middle of the road could have served as the center line if there'd been room for two cars. Declan parked the car in the entrance to a farmer's field. I slipped my navy-blue knit beret from my coat pocket and put it on. I stepped from the car, and the wind almost whisked away the cap. I placed a hand on top of my Paris souvenir, keeping it in place. A strong gust slapped hair against my face, and I tucked it behind my ear.

A rusted metal roof covered the deserted stone house. Ivy trailed across the front and entered the dwelling through the glassless windows. A weathered green wooden door hung crooked on rusted hinges. An outbuilding's stone roof lay in a pile of rubble in the middle of the structure. Declan untied a fraying rope securing the gate on an iron fence surrounding the homestead. He heaved up the gate while pushing it open, a creaking sound filling the air.

My chest fluttering, I stepped onto the same land Grandma hadn't stepped foot on since leaving Ireland in 1936. My parents lived in the house I'd grown up in. I couldn't imagine not having that home to go back to even though I wasn't thrilled to still be living there.

"It looks like one of my granny's gingerbread houses," Declan said. "Actually, *better* than most of them."

I laughed, brushing a finger over the thick, gnarly ivy vines climbing up the side of the house. Inches in diameter, they resembled tree branches. "I never knew vines could get so thick."

"Nobody has lived here since your grandma's sister Agnes died in 1985," Sadie said.

"Did it have indoor plumbing or electricity?"

"No, even at that time some houses still didn't have either."

"Did she live here by herself?"

"No man in his right mind would have married that woman," Seamus said, his jolly demeanor vanishing. "Neighborhood kids were afraid of her. When they were naughty, their parents would say, 'Ya better behave, or we'll drop you off at Agnes Coffey's.'"

So no need to bother interviewing neighbors for fond memories of Agnes.

Declan snapped a pic of Sadie, Seamus, and me in front of the house. Then, Seamus took a photo of Declan and me. I wouldn't be standing there right now if it hadn't been for Declan's help.

The door refused to open, blocked from the inside.

"Let's crawl through the window," Declan said.

The plaster framing the window had crumbled away, revealing brick and jagged-edged stones. "What if it collapses? I don't want to be responsible for destroying my family home." I peered into the dark dwelling, curious what was inside.

"It'll be fine," Declan said. "Deserted dwellings have survived hundreds of years in Ireland. They're made of sturdy stock, like our ancestors."

"I'll hold your coat, luv," Sadie said.

I slipped off my long green coat and handed it to her. Goose bumps skittered across my skin despite my heavy blue sweater. I cautiously raised a knee onto the window frame. When it didn't crumble beneath me, I lifted the other one and crawled inside. Declan followed. Leaves, soiled newspapers, and old bottles littered the dirt floor. A three-legged wooden chair leaned in a corner against the faded whitewashed walls covered in green moss. Ivy dangled from the ceiling, and clumps of straw from the original thatched roof were tucked between the wooden-pegged beams. I could envision my great-grandma Mary spinning wool by the large stone fireplace, a black kettle containing potato soup hanging over it, while the kids sat at the table doing homework, if they'd gone to school. A smaller room was attached to each end of the main one.

"How many kids were in the family?" I asked my rellies, peeking their heads in the window.

"Five," Sadie said.

"Seven people in two bedrooms?"

"There would have been a loft to climb up in and take advantage of the heat from the fireplace."

I approached the fireplace filled with leaves, twigs, and branches, as if it were waiting for someone to come home and heat up the damp interior.

"Man, how I wish these walls could talk..."

"What fun would that be?" Declan said. "Giving you all the answers and solving the mystery for ya?"

A huge black bird flew from the fireplace and swooped at us. It snatched up my knit beret. I let out a startled scream and Declan pulled me back against him. The bird escaped out the window.

"Jaysus. Are you okay?" Declan asked, his breath warm against my ear.

I stood paralyzed, unable to believe a stupid bird had just flown off with my Paris souvenir.

He curled his fingers into my trembling arms. "Take a deep breath."

I nodded, inhaling a ragged breath.

A rustling noise came from the fireplace, sounding more like a critter than a bird. I pressed my back firmly against Declan's chest. We stepped back in sync until we reached the window. I crab crawled out the window and dropped onto the ground. Declan appeared behind me.

Sadie and Seamus stood at the edge of the yard, deep in grass. A determined look on her face, Sadie glared across the back field. "Maybe the bloody thing lives in one of those trees." Massive oaks lined the drive leading up to a large stone house perched on top of a gently rolling hill.

Seamus shook his head. "He's in Mullingar by now."

Sadie's shoulders sagged in defeat, her stern look relaxing. "I'm so sorry about your hat."

I frowned. "I got it in Paris."

"I'm there next month," Declan said. "I'll go to the Eiffel Tower and get you the same one."

I smiled faintly. "Thanks." That was so sweet. Yet it wouldn't be the one I'd worn in all of our goofy Paris pictures.

Declan gazed across the field. "Does anybody live in that house?"

"It's the Daly estate," Sadie said.

Michael Daly was the groom's name on Grandma's possible marriage certificate I'd found online from a Protestant church in England.

"Did a Michael Daly live there?" I asked.

"Don't know if there was a Michael in the family or not. Didn't visit here often since me mum had a bit of a falling out with her parents over your grandmum leaving."

"Why did she leave?"

"Not sure. It was difficult for Mum to discuss. She just said there was too much sadness for her in Ireland to ever be happy. Funny the things that families discuss or don't discuss."

"I heard an older woman from Dublin comes and stays a few times a year," Seamus said.

"Is she related to the Dalys?"

Seamus shrugged his narrow shoulders. "Never hear

much about her. It's just always been known as the Daly estate."

"I could stop at the post after Christmas and see if they'll give me her Dublin address," Declan said. "She likely has her mail held or forwarded. Or we can come back and knock on neighbors' doors until we find someone who knows her."

I gave Declan an appreciative smile.

I told Sadie and Seamus about the marriage certificate.

"Was the Daly family English?" I asked.

"Aye, the family would have been of English ancestry," Seamus said. "The Dalys were once wealthy landowners, back when the English owned all the land and the Irish merely tenants. The Coffeys would have rented from the Dalys for generations. Could see how that might have caused a feud between the two families. And why they'd have had to sneak off to England to marry, then to America."

This was sounding like a historical romance novel, one of forbidden love. If Grandma had married a member of this Daly family, they'd endured a lot to be together, yet their love had persevered.

"Keep in mind, Daly is one of Ireland's most common surnames," Seamus said. "There's a Dalystown just south of here. And there were relations to this Daly family up the road at the McDonald's place and where the Doyles now live."

That put a slight damper on my enthusiasm.

"I have what I'm sure is your grandmother's wedding snap in me mother's old albums," Sadie said. "Could, of course, be of your grandfather and her, sent from the States."

My grandparents' wedding photo was displayed on Mom's bedroom dresser. When I saw Sadie's photo I'd know immediately if it was my grandpa.

I pictured the Daly homestead as having once been a grand estate that held croquet matches and fancy garden parties on the yard now buried in tall grass and neglected landscaping. The disparity between the Daly's impressive stone home and Grandma's tiny cottage clearly reflected their social standings. If she had married into this family, she must have really loved Michael to disobey her family's wishes, especially being a woman at that time. Grandma had been even more courageous than I'd thought.

Had they fought all odds to be together?

The bigger question was, what had caused them to part?

I was still chilled to the bone from the wind despite a fire roaring in the black cast-iron stove in Sadie's cozy living room. Lace doilies draped the arms of a blue-and-yellow patterned couch with a yellow crocheted blanket folded across the back. While Sadie and Seamus prepared tea in the kitchen, Declan and I snooped around.

I admired a black-and-white antique wedding photo on a shelf. "I can't wait to see my grandma's photo. It's sad how few old family pictures we have. They probably got thrown away because people didn't know who they were or they just didn't care."

"Or they got sold. My granny Byrnes collected old snaps she found in antique or charity shops or at estate sales. Didn't know who the people were, but she wanted to give them a proper home. Made her sad when people discarded a piece of their past. At least they sold them rather than putting them out with the weekly rubbish. When she died, my mum kept the snaps. Bloody boxes of them. She packed them away except for Granny's favorite. She hung it on the stairway wall."

I smiled. "I wondered why she hadn't known how that couple was related. A hundred years from now that might be a family historian's nightmare when he wonders who the hell was Uncle Thomas Flood and Catherine Darcy. And then he spends months traipsing through cemeteries and sifting through old church records trying to find a Flood family connection."

Declan laughed, nodding. "Won't help if the stories we made up about the snaps are passed down and thought true. We used to say Thomas Flood went to America and made a bloody fortune panning for gold in the West. That he sent money back to his Irish rellies so they could breed racehorses, two of which won England's Grand National. We made up some brilliant stories."

A smile curled the corners of his mouth, and his reminiscent expression reflected a deep love for his grandma. He'd once admitted his guilt over having been traveling for work when she died last year. If he'd been avoiding home after Shauna's death, he hadn't seen his grandma much the past three years.

"Sounds like she was a wonderful woman. I wish my

grandma had lived longer so I had more memories of her."

He nodded. "My mum inherited her sentimental nature, taking in strays, like her nutcracker collection."

Seamus entered the room carrying a silver tray with a china teapot and cups rattling against their saucers. With shaky hands, he set the tray on the wooden cocktail table in front of the couch.

"These teacups were part of your great-grandmum Mary's collection." Sadie placed a three-tiered china cake stand with baked goods next to the tray, then gestured to the dozens of cups on tables and shelves. "The entire lot of them."

I brushed a finger gently over a delicate white cup with green shamrocks and ivy next to the framed photo.

"My mum and her sister Ellen inherited it. Mary's dad started the Flannery china factory. It closed in the 1970s."

"Mary's last name was Flannery," I mused, studying the gold family surname logo on the bottom of the cup, the same logo that was on my teacup at home. Grandma's teacup collection had lined her windowsills. Rachel and I used to drink hot cocoa from our favorite ones.

"The factory was down near Arklow, in southern Wicklow, wasn't it?" Declan asked.

"It was," Sadie said.

"We didn't go that far south on our tour," he told me.

On Rachel's last meeting, we'd taken the group on a County Wicklow tour. Prior to it, Declan and I had discovered in the 1911 census that Mary Coffey was from there.

"We can probably find info about the factory online," Declan said. "And maybe there are still Flannerys in that area."

Declan's enthusiasm about my family research reassured me that I wasn't dragging him unwillingly to visit my rellies. A refreshing quality in a boyfriend.

"You should have that cup," Sadie said. "Take one for Rachel and your mum also."

"Oh, I couldn't take from your collection."

"Nonsense. I have no daughters, and me lads won't fancy a teacup collection. Be nice knowing they're going to a good home."

Grandma couldn't have hated her family if she'd traveled thousands of miles to America with the cups. Had her parents allowed her to take them, or had she snuck off with them in the middle of the night? What had happened to her collection after she'd died? I doubted that Mom or her sisters knew they had a tie to our family history. They'd probably been so upset after finding Grandma's letters to her supposed dead sister that they'd donated the cups to a thrift shop where they'd parted ways for a quarter each. Why hadn't Grandma told someone their sentimental value? My heart ached over the possible loss of the collection.

I selected the shamrock-and-ivy cup for myself and a sunflower one for Rachel, who'd always worn Grandma's sunflower apron, and a red-patterned one for Mom, her favorite color.

Sadie unwrapped the copies of Grandma's letters and our family photo. She brushed a finger over the red ribbon tied around the stack of letters. "'Twas a lucky thing me mum kept the envelopes your grandmum's letters came in, or my sister Catherine would never have been able to notify her when our mum passed." She set the letters on the cocktail table. "I'll read them later."

"The photo was taken at my grandma's when I was seven. It was her last Christmas. That's three generations." We were standing in front of my grandparents' tree, filled with homemade ornaments from their grandchildren.

Sadie pointed at my grandma. "My, she looks like me mother when she was older, doesn't she now?"

Seamus nodded. "Same chin."

Sadie slapped a hand against the sofa's arm. "We were going to find her wedding snap." She went over and slipped a large photo album from a bookshelf. A maroon cord bound the tattered-edged black pages within a sturdy cardboard cover. Declan and I sat on either side of her on the couch, and she paged through it, finding a black-and-white pic of Grandma in a simple yet elegant lace gown. The groom, an insanely handsome man in a dark suit, resembled a young Cary Grant with a killer smile, rather than Grandpa. In the lower right corner of its cardboard frame, a gold-embossed logo read *Fagan's, Dublin.*

"So I'm guessing that's not your grandpa if the photo was taken at a studio in Dublin," Declan said.

"No, it's not. He's also likely not Michael Daly. They wouldn't have gotten married in England and had their wedding photo taken in Dublin."

"Would have been rather odd," Sadie mused. "He

might have been a Dublin rellie of the Daly landowner and how they'd met."

Sadie slipped the photo from the corner tabs and turned it over. Scrawled on the back in faded ink was John Daly and Bridget Coffey. No year.

"Ah, brilliant," Declan said. "Now you know his name, and he was likely from Dublin."

It confirmed Grandma had indeed married an Irish gent named Daly. However, the certificate I'd found online definitely wasn't Grandma's. The story that she'd run off to England to marry her childhood sweetheart—a forbidden love—was so romantic I wanted desperately for it to be true.

Sadie handed me the photo. "Your family should have this."

I wasn't sure I wanted photographic evidence of Grandma's first marriage. It wasn't like I could frame it and set it next to my grandparents' wedding pic. Had Grandpa known about the marriage, or had she kept it a secret from him to protect his feelings, as well as her own?

I zoned in on a silver broach with emerald-colored stones on Grandma's high-collared dress. Although the pic was black and white, I knew the colors because the pin was in Mom's jewelry box. I'd once taken it without permission to play dress-up, and my mom had wigged out since she'd worn it for her wedding. Mom would really wig out that she'd worn the broach from Grandma's first marriage.

A marriage the family hadn't even known about.

CHAPTER TWELVE

"Don't be too disappointed the marriage certificate you found wasn't your granny's," Declan said, pulling out of Sadie's drive. "Knowing her husband's name was John, and likely from Dublin, is massive. How's your mum going to react to the snap?"

I stared at Grandma's wedding photo, nibbling on my lower lip. "I'm not sure if I'm going to tell her. My mom wore that same broach for her wedding."

"Ah, right, then. That could be a wee bit disturbing."

"My mom and she were never real close, and I'm afraid this is going to be pretty upsetting."

Declan reached over and placed a hand on mine. I relaxed back in the seat. Our trip had gotten off to a rough start, encountering Liam in the pub, but our relationship was getting back on track.

"You'll know when it's the right time to tell her." He slipped his hand from mine and shifted into third gear. "We'll look up the Flannery china factory when we get home and see if we can find any information."

When we get *home*.

That further calmed the uneasy feeling in my stomach over Grandma's wedding photo. I slipped it in my purse. Sadie and Seamus had offered to contact a cousin, who knew everything about their family—and everyone else's—to ask if she knew the background on Grandma's husband. Knowing I'd return in March with Rachel had made saying good-bye easier.

When we arrived at *home*, Declan's mom ushered us inside and caught the front door before the wind took it off the hinges. "I'll put the kettle on, and you can tell me all about your visit."

I swept my hair back from my eyes, no beret to contain it. "I've never been so windblown in my life."

"It's going to get worse," she said. "They're calling for gale-force winds late tonight, up to one hundred twenty kilometers per hour. They've already hit England. Hopefully, our electric stays on. Would be a shame for the yard not to light up."

Zoe came bounding down the stairs. "Would be mad to see the Grinch and his sheep flying over the pub tonight during the Christmas party."

"It would not," Jane snapped.

"Are you connecting in Heathrow?" Declan asked me.

I nodded, my heart about stopped. "You think there might be an issue with flights?"

"If the winds are fierce, they might already know if the incoming flight from the States is messed up. It's likely the same plane returning to Chicago. Do you get text alerts from the airline?"

I shook my head, unaware such a thing existed.

"We should check your flight."

I'd been worried about transferring planes by myself at one of the world's busiest airports. I'd never dreamed there might not be a plane to transfer to! I grabbed my flight info from my purse while Declan booted up the computer on a desk in the living room. We all peered anxiously over his shoulder while he accessed my reservation.

Canceled.

My stomach dropped. "They have me rebooked on a flight getting in at noon Christmas Eve day. My mom is going to freak. We spend that day preparing food for our annual party."

So much for making up for being a bad daughter the last two years. I couldn't blame this year on Andy.

Declan checked flights at Dublin airport. "It's already knackered from delays at Heathrow."

"What about another airport?" Desperation filled my voice. "Isn't there a Shauna airport?"

Jane and Zoe exchanged panicked glances.

Declan's hands froze on the keyboard, his body tense.

I'd said *Shauna* instead of *Shannon*.

Who named a flippin' airport after a girl? I had Shauna on the brain. And now Declan *knew* I had Shauna on the brain! I'd lucked out that he hadn't heard me blabbing to Rachel, but he'd definitely heard me this time.

A cow mooed in the distance. Peat crackled in the fireplace. It was as if Shauna's name hadn't been spoken in the house since her death. It undoubtedly hadn't.

My heart thumped wildly in my chest. I finally muttered, "I'm sorry."

Jane blew out a ragged breath. "It's about time we talked about her. Shauna died, but we act as if she'd never even *lived*. That isn't right."

Declan shook his head, gaze glued to the computer. "We're not discussing this right now."

"Then when?" Jane demanded.

"Not now."

"Well, I'm sorry, but I want to." Jane frowned. "You aren't the only one who loved her."

Declan shoved his chair back, the legs scratching across the wood floor. He sprang up. The look of pain in his eyes made my heart ache. Before I could extend a comforting hand, he stormed from the room. The front door slammed shut. A car hummed to life, and Declan sped out of the driveway.

"I'm so sorry," I said, staring down the hallway in shock.

"He's as stubborn as his father." Jane burst into tears and flew up the stairs.

"Fancy some tea?" Zoe asked.

Seriously?

She shrugged. "It wouldn't be Christmas without some family drama. After three years, the silence is finally broken. About time we talked about Shauna. Mum and I don't even talk about her to each other."

"Declan probably won't talk to *me* ever again." A sick feeling tossed my stomach.

"If he doesn't come back, I'll take you to the airport."

"You think he might not come back before I leave?"

"Who knows. Mum's right. He's a stubborn arse sometimes."

I went from bringing Declan home and saving their

family Christmas to ruining it. Maybe Cullens B & B still had room at their inn. If I couldn't get out of the country, I had to at least get out of this house.

I trudged outside in the duck wellies to the far end of the backyard, attempting to get cell service, steering clear of the barking-dog alarm. I also didn't want everyone to hear what would undoubtedly be more family drama when I told Mom about my flight and ruined *my* family's Christmas.

I avoided calling Mom and checked my e-mail. Bernice had sent me several links to contests she'd entered on my behalf. I clicked one, and up popped a picture of an Irish terrier puppy, a Dublin dog club giveaway. A dog? Besides the challenges of getting a dog back into the US, I'd never owned one. My last pet was our cat Izzy while growing up. Maybe Declan's parents would want a real dog rather than merely a barking alarm. I replied, thanking Bernice, debating whether to tell her I traveled too much to own a pet. If I sounded unappreciative, she might stop entering me in contests. Yet, what other crazy contests was she signing me up for?

The cold, brisk wind whipped my hair against my face, making my eyes water. I took a deep breath, inhaling the scent of freshly fallen rain and damp earth, trying to calm the icky feeling in my stomach as I called Mom. Plastering on a perky smile, I started our conversation with my visit to Sadie's house and Grandma's childhood home. I left out the part that I'd hoped it might have been next door to her husband's family estate. And that a stupid bird living in the dwelling had stolen my beret.

"Did you know your grandma Mary Coffey's family owned a teacup manufacturer, Flannerys? That's where Grandma's cups came from. She couldn't have hated her entire family to have kept the cups and traveled so far with them. Do you still have some of her collection? Mine says Flannerys on it."

"Teri kept them. With her hoarding issues, I'm sure she still has them. I'll ask her."

A sense of relief washed over me.

Mom sounded genuinely enthused and a bit intrigued for the first time since I'd started researching Grandma. Was it because she was currently on the green tea health bandwagon, or was it relief that I'd discovered Grandma's family had been china makers rather than sheep thieves?

"I was thinking I might make my mom's bread for the party."

It'd been so long since Mom had made the brown bread that my memories of its taste had long faded. Her desire to bake it was a good sign my research was bringing her closer to her mother. A sign that I shouldn't tell her the truth about Grandma's first marriage and her wedding broach.

Instead, I broke the bad news about my canceled flight.

Silence filled the line. A sheep baaed in the distance. A text alert shrilled in my ear, startling me. I pictured Mom's lips pressed into a thin line, disappointment in her eyes.

"I'm so sorry. I'll take the bus from O'Hare so nobody has to pick me up. I'll be home to help before anyone arrives. I'm sure Rachel will help out."

"I'll be fine." Her tone was matter of fact. "But what about you? Over in a strange country all by yourself?"

Grandma must have been lonely that first Christmas in America without her family or friends, if her husband hadn't immigrated with her. How difficult, moving to a new country and building relationships from scratch. However, I had few relationships in the country I'd lived in for twenty-four years.

"Sadie lives nearby if I need anything." However, she was on her way to Cork to spend the holidays with her son. "And my coworker Declan lives in the area."

That Declan was a coworker was the only thing Mom knew about him. Even though Rachel was now aware of our relationship, I still wasn't prepared to deal with Mom's concerns over my ability to choose a *nice young man* after dating Andy for two years. I was a total hypocrite, wigging out on Declan for wanting to introduce me as merely a friend to his family.

"Rachel's helping with Dad, isn't she?"

Mom was likely rolling her eyes at the thought of my sister helping out. I'd have thought the same thing a few months ago, but Rachel was changing. She'd gone home to help with Dad. Before, she'd have sent *me* home and stayed in Dublin to work on Flanagan's meeting.

"She's over at noon today," Mom said with a hint of doubt.

"I didn't do this on purpose."

"I know, dear. I have to go. Your father needs me."

Click. She was gone. I hadn't heard Dad calling out to her in the background. Was she upset, or had she really had to go? She hadn't had a meltdown, yet I was riddled with guilt. Reverse psychology. Act fine to make me feel even worse. Why couldn't I just be happy that she hadn't started crying?

The text alert shrilled again.

Rachel, wondering about my visit with Sadie.

Emotionally drained, I had zero energy for another conversation. However, Mom might direct her anger at Rachel, blaming her for my job, the canceled flight, and Ireland's unpredictable weather. I had to warn my sister so she wasn't blindsided. And this was our journey. I wanted to share it with her. I called Rachel and recounted my visit with Sadie and promised to e-mail a picture of Grandma's home and her wedding photo. I told her Grandma's hubby's name was John, not Michael, and he'd likely lived in Dublin, not the son of a wealthy landowner next door to Grandma.

Rachel gasped. "How mysterious and romantic would that have been?"

My sister never romanticized anything. I'd bawled through the movie *Ghost* despite Rachel droning on about the improbability of the afterlife and Whoopi Goldberg's psychic abilities.

"Why'd she keep the marriage a secret?" she said. "I wonder if Grandpa even knew. They married in 1947, eleven years after she immigrated. What did she do all those years?"

"I'm not saying anything to Mom until I know the entire story. She's already upset that I'm not getting home now until Christmas Eve day, thanks to gale-force winds."

"Oh shit. I bet she freaked out."

"She was actually eerily calm about it."

"She's probably popping Teri's anxiety meds, with everything going on."

"That would explain it. Can you help her get ready for the party?"

"Of course. Did you get an extra night at the B and B?"

After keeping Declan a secret, I had to tell Rachel the truth. I couldn't risk damaging our relationship any further.

"I'm staying at Declan's. His parents are home. His mother insisted." I sounded like a teenager justifying a sleepover at a girlfriend's house. "But don't tell Mom."

"Oh, okay."

I wasn't sure if she sounded surprised that I'd shared this information with her or that my relationship with Declan was more serious than she'd thought.

"I hope it goes well."

I admitted that it *wasn't* going particularly well since I'd blurted out Shauna's name.

"Wow, that sucks. I'm so sorry." Rachel sounded sympathetic and genuinely concerned. "Call me if you need to talk."

"Thanks. I will." I smiled, relieved that I hadn't totally effed up our relationship.

"Oh, and Gerry Coffey called me last night."

"What did he want?"

"To talk. He'd come to the hotel to say good-bye, but I'd already left."

How romantic was that?

"He wants to get together in March."

"Do you want to?"

"Yeah, it might be fun to hook up when I'm in town."

Is that what Declan and I were doing? Hooking up when we were on site together? Rachel didn't sound like she'd meant to imply that, but the thought had popped into my head...

A flash of red and green ran down the road beyond the yard. I squinted in the distance. "I have to go. There's...sheep, I think, in the road." What *I* was going to do about it, I had no clue. However, if Declan returned driving like a maniac, he might hit them.

Declan had once explained that bright splashes of color on sheep's cream wool coats helped designate ownership if they wandered off. These sheep were fully dyed, looking like they were wearing Christmas sweaters. I traipsed across the lawn, my feet sinking into the squishy grass and soil. I joined Zoe on the road, thirty feet from the sheep. No cars coming, I snapped a quick pic of the animals staring at us.

"What should we do?" I whispered.

"Walk slowly toward them and baa quietly. It calms them."

I took a cautious step forward. "Baaaaa."

Their dark eyes watched my every move.

I leaned over, bracing my hands on my knees, at eye level with the animals. "Baaaa." My voice grew louder. Looking a tad freaked out, they trotted over to a low-lying fence area and jumped back into the field.

"Oh, hi, Carrig," Zoe said.

I turned to find a guy, thirtyish, in jeans and a

flannel jacket, giving me a curious stare. "A sheep whisperer, are ya?"

"Um, I was just trying to get them out of the road."

"Ah, a Yank." He nodded as if me being American explained my bizarre behavior.

Zoe burst out laughing. She'd set me up, knowing this guy was heading over to round up his sheep. Yet I was still proud of myself for herding sheep off the road and into the field, possibly saving their lives.

The guy shook his head. "You're both mad as the arse who dyed my sheep. Would guess it was Declan if he still lived here."

Zoe rolled her eyes. "Calm down. We're just having some craic."

"Ah, great craic, is it? When I find the wanker who did this, I'm going to *crack* his head and decorate his lawn with sheep shite." He stormed off, cussing.

"Declan and he don't fancy each other. Goes back to fourth grade and Megan McDuffy. And when Declan was ten, he painted Carrig's favorite sheep with a lovely Monet landscape."

"Omigod. What did your parents do?"

"Told him it was brilliant. They've always encouraged his art. He didn't realize the practical purpose for the dye. He thought their wool was a blank canvas for painting."

A sheep was nosing around by the lowered fence, planning its escape route.

"Hey, get baaaaack from that fence," I said.

It trotted off into the field.

Zoe laughed. "Fair play to ya. You're now an official sheepherder. Like Heidi in the Alps. Or more like, Caity on the Bog. Maybe you could have your own reality TV show."

"Oh yeah, I'd love the entire world watching me baa like a crazy person at sheep."

I gazed out over the rolling hills, imagining pastel-painted sheep resembling an Impressionist landscape. I could herd the sheep, and Declan could paint them. Living a simpler, stress-free life where I didn't have to worry about massive debt and contracting my next job, merely spinning our colorful wool into stylish sweaters shipped around the world. However, learning to spin wool likely required good coordination skills. Maybe we could dye their wool for every holiday and our pictures would go viral on social media, earning us millions.

Upon returning to the house, Zoe ran to her room, and I went to the kitchen to make a cup of tea. There was something comforting about the saying *I'll put the kettle on.* Yet I wondered if many people still heated an actual kettle on the stove. A flip of the switch and the plastic pitcher plugged into the wall was soon whistling, steam rising from its spout. I selected a yellow ceramic mug from the white cupboards and added water and a teabag. I sat at the table topped with a blue-and-white gingham cloth, which matched the curtains. I relaxed, sipping the warm golden beverage, peering out the window at the backyard stretching toward a tree line in the distance.

Zoe flew into the room, holding up a red sweater

with a Christmas tree decorated in miniature lights. "You can wear this to the pub party tonight. Try it on."

It was hideous. However, Zoe was bubbling with enthusiasm, and a party might put me back in the holiday spirit, so I reluctantly slipped on the sweater.

"It looks fab. But here's the best part." She pressed a small button on the sweater's inside, and the tree lit up. She pushed another, and "Rockin' Around the Christmas Tree" began playing. "You can also make the lights flash."

How about making them turn *off*?

Jane walked in and smiled at the goofy sweater. Thank God she wasn't staying locked away in her bedroom, avoiding me and the holidays.

"I see Zoe sucked you into the ugly jumper contest at the pub tonight."

My gaze darted to Zoe. "So you think this sweater's ugly?"

Her top lip curled back. "It's bloody awful."

If Andy could only see me now. Last Christmas we'd attended a friend's party at an upscale downtown hotel and I'd had to lose five pounds to fit into a red designer dress he'd intentionally bought a size too small. He'd had such a fit over my "tacky" jingle bell earrings that he'd given me my present early—the Tiffany diamond studs I'd sold on Craigslist. Despite all the compliments, I'd been bummed about not wearing the festive earrings that jingled every time I moved my head.

"I'll wear it," I said.

"Brilliant."

"What about you?"

"Be right back." Zoe flew upstairs and returned wearing a green sweater with Jesus in a red party hat and a white tunic that read *Birthday Boy*.

"Take that thing off," Jane demanded. "It's blasphemy."

"Why? It's His birthday, isn't it?"

"Wearing that to an ugly jumper contest is disrespectful. What if Father Doyne is at the pub? Now take it off, and go to the store for me. I need to make party treats, and I forgot the green grapes for the Grinch kabobs."

"I should bring something," I said.

Zoe's face lit up. "How about egg nog? They're always drinking it in American movies, like *National Lampoon's Christmas Vacation*. I'm dying to try it."

"I make it for our family party. I have the recipe memorized."

"That'd be brill."

I gave Zoe the list of ingredients and twenty euros. "That should cover it. I'll buy the rum from the pub."

"Yum, rum." Zoe licked her lips. "I knew I'd love egg nog."

"I can stay and help you," I told Jane.

"That'd be lovely."

"Leave the reindeer pops for me to make." Zoe whisked out the back door.

Jane glared at her daughter for not having changed the sweater. "A bit cheeky, isn't she?"

I smiled. "I have to warn you—I'm not exactly Betty Crocker." I wanted to ask if their homeowner's insurance premium was paid but didn't want to worry her. "As long as we aren't making goose, I should be okay."

Jane's nose crinkled in disgust. "I'd never make goose."

Deciding she needed some cheering up, I shared my goose curry debacle.

She laughed. "Well, it's a good thing I'm not making my curry dip or curry cheese melts. Can you stick a marshmallow, banana slice, and strawberry on a toothpick?"

"I can handle that." How much damage could a toothpick cause? I'd thought the same thing about a baster.

"Grand. I'll have you start on the Santa kabobs."

Jane placed wooden cutting boards on the white countertop. I stuck big soft marshmallows on the end of several dozen toothpicks while Jane sliced chunks of bananas for Santa's face.

"There'll be melted chocolate for dipping. Light and dark. Declan only fancies dark." She frowned. "If he's home for the party..."

"I'm sorry again about before."

"No worries. It's not your fault. We never should have gone so long without talking about Shauna. At first I honored Declan's need to not discuss her because it was too painful. Then, he rarely came home, and the longer we went without talking about her, the more difficult it became. When he was only home a day or two, I didn't wish to upset him, afraid he'd stop coming home. But we all stopped talking about her, and that's not right."

I totally got it. I hadn't even been able to utter Andy's name out loud to *myself* for months after our breakup. Since confiding in Rachel and Declan about him, I'd lost three pounds cutting back on comfort food and was sleeping through the night without meds. Martha would advise me to encourage the family to discuss Shauna. That it wasn't healthy keeping problems bottled up inside. If I couldn't help Declan heal, maybe I could help his family so they'd be in a better place to help him.

"I'm just afraid he's closed himself off to ever loving again." Jane was slicing the bananas with excessive force. My bagel incident flashed through my mind.

I wanted to confess that Declan and I were more than friends, give her a glimmer of hope to not give up on him—and to not lose a finger.

And to remind *myself* not to give up on him.

"In Paris, we took the group to a cemetery, and he broke down and told me about Shauna."

Jane smiled, setting down the knife. "That's probably the first time he's talked to *anyone* about her."

She didn't appear hurt that he'd confided in me when he was incapable of saying Shauna's name to family. I wouldn't tell her that he'd also made me promise to never bring her up again.

"He admitted avoiding his emotions since her death. That it was easier to just stop feeling, period." Although he hadn't promised to start *expressing* his feelings, I'd assumed he would after our kiss.

Declan was going to flip out that I'd told his mom this. Yet it also affected me, and I needed to talk about it.

Jane gave me a hug. "Don't give up on him. I fear I had." She drew back, smiling. "Come here."

I followed her down the hallway. She snatched a framed family Christmas photo off the credenza and marched up the stairs. With a defiant look, she hung the picture on the empty nail and let out a whoosh of air.

"I feel like a dark cloud has finally passed after hovering over our house for three years. You probably think it's silly that hanging a snap there is such a big deal."

Not at all. That empty nail had been haunting me since I'd arrived. Yet how was Declan going to react?

"Shauna loved the holidays. We're going to honor her memory by celebrating it, not ignoring it." She smiled with determination. "Whether he's home for it or not."

She also believed Declan might not return before I left?

He obviously had a track record of running off, and it didn't seem to faze anyone except me. I'd never seen this selfish side of him, and I didn't like it. He was no longer merely emotionally avoiding his feelings, but now *physically* avoiding them. I didn't want a guy who ran away from his problems, especially now that I was learning to face mine.

CHAPTER THIRTEEN

Carter's pub was only a half mile from Declan's parents. We walked single file on a narrow strip of grass bordering the side of the road. My flashing sweater and Colin's and Jane's yellow reflective vests cautioned vehicles to slow down. I hoped my sweater wasn't distracting enough to cause a driver to run off the road and into a sheep field. Carrying the food containers, glass punch bowl, and sloshing egg nog-filled pitchers wasn't easy when struggling to walk against the forceful winds. However, Colin was too afraid to risk a drunk-driving ticket.

A group of men stood smoking outside the white pub with blue-framed windows. One of them eyed the creamy beverage in my glass pitcher. "Milk, is it? Jane gotcha off the whiskey, does she?" he asked Colin.

"It's egg nog," Colin said. "An American tradition."

"Made with alcohol, so you'll fancy it, Daniel," Jane said.

The men raised their pints, wishing us a happy holiday as we walked inside.

A small dog in a red Santa sweater sat on a barstool next to an elderly man. Another slept curled up under a table. Several kids were dancing to "Jingle Bell Rock," sung by two musicians on stools next to a decorated tree. Coal burned in the brick fireplace despite the body heat warming the small pub. Rather than horse races, a dart championship was playing on TV. Besides Jane in her plain red sweater and Colin in a green reindeer tie, red and green sports jerseys were more popular than festive sweaters.

I eyed Zoe in her red reindeer sweater and antlers headband. "Thought this was a contest?"

"I'm trying to get people in the spirit of the ugly jumper."

I turned off my flashing sweater, reminded of the time Declan and I had been the only ones dressed in Halloween costumes at a trendy Paris lounge. Declan had looked way hot in the pilot's uniform, and the flight attendant costume had given me a boost of self-esteem, making me feel worldly and envied by others. However, right now I'd rather be here in this rural pub than jetting off to Bangkok or Venice.

I wasn't sure if I should be worried that Declan might have gotten in an accident after driving off like a lunatic. Or maybe he took off for another country. He probably had enough hotel points to hide out until summer. Part of me wanted to call him, and the other part said *he* should call *me*. And what if he didn't answer my call? I was leaving in another day, and he wouldn't see me again until... I didn't know when, now that my February Venice program had canceled. It apparently bothered me more than it did him. Which bothered me even more.

Carrig, who owned the Christmas sheep, stood with a group of buddies dressed in soccer jerseys and T-shirts, drinking pints. They eyed me with curiosity, either admiring my unique fashion sense or questioning the sanity of the crazy Yank wandering their roads baaing at sheep.

"Where's your feckin' brother?" one of them asked Zoe.

"Didn't feel like being involved in any of your shenanigans, Darragh Reilly. He's more mature now." She looked over at me. "*He's* probably the one who painted Carrig's sheep. He and Declan used to get into some fierce trouble."

"Like stealing the Guinness truck?"

"Yeah, they were quite the pair. But that Darragh is gorgeous, isn't he? Too bad he's engaged to Breeda." She gave her eyes an exaggerated roll.

Zoe knew everybody in the place. I'd never known my neighbors at my downtown condo. I hadn't realized the woman across the hall had died until a new owner moved in a month later. I didn't know any of my parents' newer neighbors.

A teenage girl wearing a Santa stocking cap came around selling raffle tickets for a charity providing toys to underprivileged children. I bought twenty-euros worth and stuffed them in a canister for a gift basket containing a bottle of Jameson, a Jameson T-shirt, whiskey glasses, whiskey fudge, and whiskey marmalade. It reminded me of the Irish gift basket I'd devoured last meeting in Dublin, before learning I'd received an attendee's gift by mistake. Yet this one would make a perfect gift for Declan.

Even though he didn't deserve one, making everyone worry.

Des and Mags Carter were third-generation publicans, running their ancestors' business. Des gave me a deal on a bottle of rum to mix with the egg nog in a punch bowl. I ladled the frothy beverage into cups and lined them up on the bar for people to taste. I offered one to an elderly man who'd been sitting at the bar watching me prepare the drink. He had on a dark suit, red tie, and reindeer slippers. A plaid flannel cap topped his wooden cane resting against the bar.

He sniffed the glass. "Egg nog, is it?"

I nodded. "You've had it before?"

"Certainly have." He took a sip. "It's quite tasty, luv."

He took another sip, closing his eyes, smiling. "Brings back memories, it does." He opened his eyes. "Memories of a lovely lass just outside Boston."

I gave him an intrigued smile.

"I worked in Boston for three years. The only time I haven't lived up the road in my parents' house."

"She must have been quite the woman."

"A true lady. Would still be there if she hadn't broken my heart."

Seemed to be a lot of that going around.

"So what brings a young lass like yourself here from the States?"

I told him about my Coffey ancestors in Killybog and how I'd hoped my Grandma had been married to her Daly neighbor.

"The landowners?" he asked.

I nodded.

"I surely have information on the family. They owned most of the land in the area. Of course, the shooting at their Killybog estate gave them historical infamy."

My gaze narrowed. "Shooting?"

"In the 1880s, a plot to shoot the landowner went bad. His sister was mistakenly killed instead while returning from church in a covered carriage. Five men were sent to prison. Supposedly more were involved in the conspiracy, but not enough evidence to bring them up on charges."

One hadn't been a Coffey, had it?

"I'm a bit of a local historian, Nicholas Turney. If you'd like, you may call down to my house tomorrow, and I'll find the story and whatever else I might have on the family."

"That'd be wonderful."

Sadie would have mentioned the murder if our ancestor had been involved, wouldn't she have? If she'd known. Or maybe she was trying to hide skeletons in our family closet. Our fear that Grandma's supposedly dead family members had been sheep thieves or petty criminals paled in comparison to having been murderers. And a Daly certainly wouldn't have married into the family responsible for murdering his rellie.

We left the pub shortly after midnight. Luckily, my

sweater was lit up because *I* was lit. I'd never had so many people I didn't know buy me drinks. The Jameson basket weighted me down, so the wind didn't whisk me away, though it made my staggering appear even worse. When we arrived home, nobody commented on the fact that Declan's car wasn't in the drive. Upset and disappointed, I gave his parents the whiskey basket as a thank-you for their warm hospitality and a silent apology for causing so much drama at the holidays.

Zoe and Colin went to bed while Jane and I sat in the living room, taste testing the whiskey fudge. Luckily, the chocolate flavor prevailed over the liquor. Lying on the back of the couch, Quigley poked his nose over my shoulder and sniffed the fudge as I took a bite. Unimpressed, he laid his head back down and dozed off, looking cozy and a bit like Elmer Fudd, in his red knit hat with ear flaps on the sides.

I studied the painting of a little girl hanging a star on a Christmas tree, next to the fireplace. "Did Declan paint that?"

Jane shook her head. "I took his paintings down after Shauna passed. They met while taking an art class. Declan was a model." Her gaze narrowed. "Wasn't naked or anything. The assignment had been to capture a realistic portrait of the model. Shauna drew a caricature instead in bright colors accenting Declan's blue eyes and exaggerating his mischievous grin. She gave it to him and said, 'That's how I see ya, Declan Grady. You're a real *character*.'" Her reminiscent smile faded. "He certainly was."

"He still is," I reassured her.

I recounted several of the funny tales Declan had shared about his work mishaps to make me feel better and not so inept. How his stories and upbeat attitude had helped me survive the start of a very difficult job.

Jane laughed softly. "Ah, thank you for that." She sprang from the couch. A bit tipsy, she steadied herself. "Be right back." She went upstairs and returned with two paintings and handed me one. "He's a brilliant artist. So sad he gave it up. You keep that. Zoe mentioned you two were out herding Carrig's sheep from the road today."

In the painting, sheep grazed on rolling hills, a lamb and its mum the focal point. A stone house sat on a ridge in the distance. Not a cloud in the blue sky. It was the field across the road. *D. Grady* was scrawled in the lower right corner.

"This is wonderful, but I can't take your painting."

Could I, when Declan refused to discuss his muse, Shauna? Would he want me hanging the painting in my bedroom when he wouldn't allow his parents to hang it on the wall?

"Nonsense. It's a gift. You can't refuse a gift. It's the perfect fit for your hand luggage."

She replaced the painting on the wall with Declan's. The scene transported me to their home on a starry night, washed in a haze of blue and white hues, streams of smoke rising from the chimney. A warm, cozy feeling wrapped around me.

When Declan returned, the house would be decorated with reminders of Shauna, and he'd have me to blame. Yet maybe his family would have me to *thank*.

I lay in bed, thinking about my encounter with the local historian, Nicholas Turney. What if an article identified a Coffey as having been brought up on murder charges but not convicted? At least he wouldn't have been found guilty. Bernice and Gracie had said they wouldn't want to know about a killer in their family unless it had been a famous one who used his powers for good rather than evil, like James Bond. Maybe that Daly landowner had been a horrible slum lord, charging outrageous rent for squalor dwellings, evicting people when they couldn't pay. Yet that didn't justify attempting to shoot him and murdering his sister.

Feeling like I'd been lying wide awake for hours, I glanced over to check the time on my phone. The empty charger lay on the nightstand. I hauled my butt out of bed and padded across the cold wood floor. After grabbing my cell phone from my purse, I placed a hand against the iron wall register, as cold as the floor. With the high cost of fuel, they must have turned off the heat at night. I slipped back under the green-and-red quilt, into the warm bed. I plugged the phone in, and a text popped up from Declan, received five hours ago while I'd been downing egg nog in the noisy pub. Nobody else had mentioned getting one. Maybe they hadn't seen theirs either.

He promised he'd be home tomorrow. He'd driven off to calm down, no destination in mind, and had hit a pothole, blowing a tire and causing a rattling under the hood. Of course, he didn't tell his whereabouts so someone could drive over and assist him. I wasn't sure if he was being honest about the flat tire. He'd better be telling the truth about being home tomorrow. I was ticked, yet my heart ached, picturing him lying in bed alone in a hotel room, even though it was his own fault. He was likely still awake. Checking on him might help me sleep. And I didn't want him to think I'd ignored his text.

I texted him. *How are you?*

My screen went black before a text popped up and a loud shrill filled the air. I turned my phone to vibrate.

Grand. How was the pub party? Great craic?

Yep. Met Nicholas Turney. Going to visit him tomorrow.

Ah, brilliant. He might be a help with your research.

While I debated how to explain the possible Coffey murder connection in a nutshell, another text popped up.

Sorry I'm not there. Will rent a car if need. Good night.

Guess that was the end of our conversation.

Good night.

At least he'd apologized. And his comment about renting a car was reassuring. But he should have called, and earlier. I verified that the only missed call I had was from Sadie. I checked her message to learn her cousin didn't have any further info on Grandma's husband or the Dalys.

Another dead end.

I peered over at Declan's painting on the white dresser, leaning against the wall. I snuggled under the quilt, imagining that warm sunny day, a light breeze carrying the baaing of sheep through the rural countryside. I pictured Declan painting at an easel, me admiring his artwork while relaxing in a white wicker chair, sipping lemonade. I had on a white floppy-brimmed hat and lace dress, and he wore a flannel cap, white linen shirt, and dark pants, like a scene out of the 1930s, Grandma's era.

I turned off the lamp, yet the idyllic, peaceful setting remained in my thoughts as I drifted off to sleep...

Chapter Fourteen

Lying in bed the following morning, I had the strange feeling someone was watching me. I cracked an eyelid to find Zoe standing over me in blue flannel jammies, her blond hair pulled up in a crooked ponytail, mascara smudges under her bloodshot eyes. She didn't look bad for having put away more pints than Carrig, the sheep guy, had.

"Brilliant, you're awake." She plopped down on the bed.

My stomach tossed from too much egg nog and hard cider. She scooched me over with her butt. I sat up against the padded headboard.

"Come with me to the Christmas market at the mall. My granny Grady and auntie Fiona are at my uncle's in Limerick for Christmas. Told them I'd work their booth. I'll go mad talking to Quigley all morning."

"Quigley works the booth with you?"

"He models the hats and ties."

"Ah, okay."

"Fab. I also need to buy Declan's gift. We always buy each other some crazy pressie. Even though he doesn't deserve one for making everyone worry about him."

Zoe obviously hadn't received a text from Declan. I told her about mine, and his excuse.

She rolled her eyes. "Feckin' liar. Flat tire my arse."

That had been my reaction.

"I'll tell Mum. She tries to act like she's not worrying, but she is." She let out a frustrated growl. "Did you tell him that he better be home in time for you to open his pressie?"

"Declan bought me a gift?"

"It's under the tree."

I couldn't believe Declan had bought me something more than the four backpacks. I shouldn't have given his parents the whiskey gift basket. Yes, I should have, after they invited me into their home and I'd caused so much drama. Besides, Declan spent a lot of time and thought putting together those backpacks. I had to get him something with meaning, despite how upset I was with him. It might help soften the blow when he saw a photo hanging where his engagement pic once had.

"Since you're leaving tomorrow, we want you to open our gifts tonight."

Our *gifts*? I didn't have a gift for anyone.

"We'll have another gift opening when Aidan is home Christmas Eve. Too bad he won't be here for you to meet."

"Bloody hell!" Jane yelled out downstairs.

Zoe and I raced down to see what was the matter. Just like in *'Twas the Night before Christmas*, minus all of Jane's cussing. She was glaring out the living room window, mouth gaping. Decorations had been blown across the yard, and one of the wire sheep was inappropriately straddling another.

Zoe laughed. "Lucky there aren't lambs running around the yard."

Jane gave her a stern look. "It isn't funny. The wind couldn't have done such a thing. Someone had too many pints at the pub last night."

Carrig and his buddies?

"Fair play to the bloke when being so knackered. And no worries. If there were lambs, Caity could herd them for you. She's a sheep whisperer, ya know."

Jane was too busy wiggin' out to question my telepathic ability to communicate with sheep. "The bloody wind is ruining my decorations."

"We can drive past Tara Gavigan's," Zoe said. "I'm sure her decorations are a wreck."

Jane's frown slowly curled into a devious smile, resembling the Grinch's.

"We'll nail the yokes to the ground if we have to." Zoe stuffed her blue-socked feet into a pair of yellow-flowered wellies and slipped a purple jacket on over her jammies. She handed me the yellow wellies with an orange beak and googly eyes.

"Are these ducks or geese?" I asked.

Zoe shrugged. "Ducks, I would think."

I slipped on the boots and my green coat. I headed outside in my jammies. It'd been years since I'd even run out to the mailbox in my pj's. However, my green Coffey T-shirt and green-and-red plaid leggings looked more like workout clothes than pj's.

Jane marched over to the mating sheep. She tugged

on the top one, but the practical joker had bent its back legs to hold it in place. Between the three of us, we finally separated the sheep. The Grinch's sleigh had blown over, poor Max crushed and deflated beneath it. The wreath from the front door had apparently whizzed across the drive like a Frisbee and landed on Zoe's car hood.

Zoe let out a squeal. "Where's my reindeer nose?" Unconcerned about any scratches from the wreath, she dropped to the ground and searched under the car for the nose.

Jane threw her arms up in frustration. "The entire lot is a bloody mess. I'm not about to haul everything over to Uncle Martin's barn to store. The winds will die down. We'll bring them inside for now."

"The house?" Zoe asked, popping up from the drive with the red reindeer nose.

"Back in the day, families shared their homes with their livestock. At least these sheep can't shite on the floor."

Had Grandma shared her tiny three-room cottage with cows and sheep besides six family members?

By the time we'd hauled all the lawn decorations inside, I was blown to bits and fuming that Declan wasn't here helping. At work, his dad had a valid excuse. The six wire sheep barely fit in my room. I nearly had one for a sleeping companion but stuck my suitcase under the bed to make space for it in a corner. I squeezed my way out of the room, encountering Zoe at the top of the stairs, struggling to hold on to the blow-up Grinch.

"I know right where this is going." She wore a sly grin. "Declan's room."

I laughed. Appropriate. However, Declan probably wouldn't find it as funny as Zoe and I did.

"Here, let me help you."

"I'm grand." She nodded toward the sheep poking its head from my room. "Put that yoke in his room so you can close your door."

I lugged the sheep down the hallway, my heart racing at the thought of what I might find in Declan's room. Hurling awards, whiskey bottle collection, posters of his favorite bands...

Who were his favorite bands?

Zoe opened the door, and we entered. A pink lace duvet lay in a pile at the foot of the bed. The pink sheets thrown back, the shape of Declan's body was molded into the mattress. My breathing quickened at the thought of him lying there naked or merely in a pair of briefs... Did he wear briefs or boxers?

"You can set that down," Zoe said.

I was still hugging the sheep. I placed it next to the Grinch on the pink rug covering the wood floor, next to a pink velvet chair.

"Did he decorate the room himself?" I asked, disappointed that frilly furnishings had replaced Declan's belongings.

Zoe laughed. "Mum made it into a guest room when he moved out. He still has some clothes and stuff in the closet." She slid her gaze toward the closet door. "He bought a wooden picture frame for Shauna with their wedding date on it. It's still wrapped at the back of the top shelf."

My gaze narrowed on the closet door.

"After it sat there for a year, I was dying to know

what it was, so I opened it. I know that was a ghastly thing to do, but I couldn't help myself. Wished I hadn't. I sat on his bed and bawled. I wrapped it back up so he'd never know."

Was the gift another sign Declan wasn't healing or that he had a crappy memory and had forgotten about it?

"Don't tell him. I've never told anyone this. You probably think I'm awful."

I shook my head. I loved that Zoe was sharing a secret she hadn't even told her best friend. I missed the gossip and camaraderie with girlfriends. I hoped Zoe followed through on her promise to visit and that we stayed in touch via Facebook and e-mail. It sucked that she lived four thousand miles away. Although, I now had enough frequent flyer miles for a one-way ticket to Dublin. A few more international meetings and I'd have enough for a round trip.

"She was the only steady girlfriend he ever had. They started dating when he was seventeen. Before that, Mum was sure he was gay. Especially after the whole Barbie doll thing. Which of course she'd have been fine with, but can you imagine Declan gay? How mad is that?"

Quite mad. Our "relationship" was only Declan's second one. He and Shauna had been together nine years. That was a huge chunk of Declan's life I might never know anything about.

Was I okay with that?

"You're fired. You're seriously the worst model

ever." Zoe flicked a fingertip against the top of Quigley's knit Santa stocking cap.

The animal's whiskers twitched, yet his eyes remained closed, his head resting on a stack of caps on the table.

"Sorry," Zoe told the woman browsing the inventory with her daughters. "He doesn't perform on demand."

I'd never seen Quigley perform, *period*.

The woman gave Zoe a sympathetic smile. "We have three at home. We'll take one for each." Her two little girls selected Christmas presents for their family pets. The woman promised to hand out Zoe's business cards at her next book club meeting.

Zoe and I were one of several dozen vendors displaying Christmas gifts, treats, and decorations outside familiar mall stores such as Penneys and TK Maxx—the equivalent of TJ Maxx back home. A train chugged around a Christmas tree inside a store window, and the mannequins in a trendy clothing shop wore glittery gold and silver party dresses.

"Besides the Christmas pudding for us, I bought this for Declan when I ran to the loo." Zoe snagged a paper bag from under the table and slipped out a flask with a deranged-looking sheep dressed as an elf that read *Eweltide Cheer*. "Think he'll like it?"

I nodded. "If he can drink whiskey from it, he'll like it."

"The sheep looks quite mad. Would go well with my mum's nutcrackers. It's perfect. The year Kate and William got married, Declan gave me wine stoppers. One with William dressed in his red Irish Guards uniform, and Kate in her lovely lace wedding dress. I absolutely adore William and Kate."

"Me too. I have like every magazine about their wedding. And I got up insanely early to watch it." I eyed the table across from us selling customized ornaments. "My mom and sister would love an ornament painted with our Coffey name and Killybog."

At least, I hoped Mom would love one. It suddenly dawned on me I hadn't heard from either my sister or Mom in almost twenty-four hours. No text, e-mail, or call checking up on me. Strange. Was Mom upset and had me on Ignore status?

"I need to give my mom a quick call."

I stepped away and phoned her, acting nonchalant, not like *I* was now checking up on *her*.

"Sorry I haven't called," she said in a rushed tone. "Just a lot going on here. Pulling molasses cookies out of the oven right now. Rachel ran to the store for a few things I forgot to pick up, including beer. Your father is cranky as hell. If he hadn't polished off that bag of beer cheese curds, it could have held him over. He shouldn't be drinking anyway with all of his pain meds. How's it going there?"

"Ah, it's going well. At a Christmas market right now with my friend Zoe."

"Oh, how nice you have a friend there. Did you remember your father's beer?" she yelled out to Rachel. She heaved an exasperated sigh. "That's right. You can't buy alcohol until after eight, and it's only seven. They need to change that law for the holidays. What happened to Milwaukee being the beer city, for God's sake?"

I wasn't sure if she was still talking to Rachel. "Uh, Mom?"

"Sorry, dear. Could I call you back later?"

"Sure, but don't worry if you don't have time. I was just checking in."

"Okay. Thanks. Love you." Click.

I was relieved Mom didn't have time to worry about me, yet it felt strange.

The vendor promised to have my ornaments ready before we closed our booth early afternoon. While placing the order for Mom's and Rachel's ornaments, the perfect one for Declan popped into my head. Sentimental yet funny.

I joined Zoe and Quigley back at the table.

"Your mum grand?" Zoe asked.

I nodded faintly. "Yeah, she sounded fine, considering everything going on." I filled Zoe in on the craziness at home. "Guess she doesn't have time to worry about me. Which is great, just weird."

"Brilliant. Now she knows you can survive on your own." She placed Declan's gift back under the table. "If he isn't home today, he's not getting it. Such a wanker, making everyone worry. Love him loads, but he's always been a bit selfish."

"I've never seen this side of him before."

I told Zoe about his acts of kindness with the backpack presents, always tipping the hotel maids to leave extra toiletries for Martha's women's shelter, and constantly coming to my rescue.

"Wow. That was an awfully nice pressie."

"He was doing it for the women, not just me."

Zoe wore a skeptical look. "He's donated a few quid to whatever charity the pub's promoting, but nothing like those backpacks. And he helped you give them away. I've never known Declan to get directly involved in a cause before. I think you're good for him. He forgot my birthday last year, but this year I got a card and a call. And he rang me again a few weeks later." Her smile faded. "He seemed to be better, but after yesterday, I'm not so sure."

"Declan and I kissed," I blurted out, wanting to give Zoe hope that Declan was healing. And I'd been dying to confide in someone about the kiss.

Zoe let out a squeal of excitement. "I knew it. Tell me all about it."

I took an encouraging breath. "It was at the Musée d'Orsay in Paris." A rush of heat warmed my neck and cheeks as I recalled, and fantasized about, Declan's lips touching mine, his arms around my waist, my hands running through his hair...

"At an art museum in Paris? How utterly romantic is that?"

"Until we got kicked out."

"Don't people make out in public all the time in Paris?"

I shrugged.

"Getting kicked out makes it seem so...forbidden. Like a romantic liaison..." Zoe swooned. "Even if it was with my brother. So how'd it happen?"

I recounted the story I'd told Jane, about how Declan had confessed avoiding his emotions after Shauna's death.

Declan's voice shouted at the back of my head. *Feckin' A, Caity. What the bloody hell are you doing telling my family 'bout us!*

Panicked, I said, "I'm not the only girl he's kissed since Shauna." And we hadn't kissed since Dublin.

"You're the only one he's cared about."

"Why do you say that?"

"Number one, he could never care about that wicked Gretchen stalker on Facebook. Number two, I can tell by the way he sometimes acts nervous around you. Like he cares what you think, when Declan has never given a shite what people think and has always done as he pleases."

"If he cares what I think, then why has he been MIA for the past day?"

"He's embarrassed about acting like an idiot and doesn't want to face you now."

"I don't think Declan being gone is about *me*." However, it was *thanks* to me. "When he does come home, you can't tell him, or anyone, that I told you about us kissing."

Zoe zipped her pinched fingers across her lips.

I wasn't sure I could trust her to keep the secret. Not that she'd intentionally blab, but I hadn't blabbed on purpose to Rachel either. It still felt good to tell someone. Besides, if Declan hadn't run off, I wouldn't be sharing all of our secrets. If he wasn't going to open up, I'd open up for him. And for me. I didn't want to keep everything inside again like I had after Andy. Like Declan's mom said, the longer you kept from saying something, the harder it was to say.

Blurting out Shauna's name had me spilling my guts.

It felt great.

Unless Declan found out.

Zoe popped up from her chair. "Feck. Where's Quigley?" Her panicked gaze darted through the crowd.

"Little shite hasn't opened his eyes once today, and now he runs off?"

My heart raced. It was Henry all over again!

"Don't worry. When I lost Henry, I found him within ten minutes."

"Was he your cat?"

"Ah, no, he was a little kid I was babysitting, in Paris."

Zoe's eyes widened with horror.

"Technically, *I* didn't lose *him*. He ran off. Like Quigley."

"I've had him since I was fourteen. We have to find him."

We flew through the market, searching everywhere for the cat. The one place we didn't look—under *our* table. We zipped past the table, and there sat Quigley on a stack of caps, cleaning Zoe's Christmas pudding from his whiskers. Several shoppers were admiring his precious Santa cap and browsing the stock.

"You're grounded." Zoe shook a scolding finger at the cat, then hugged it. She reached under the table and grabbed the half-eaten, cake-like pudding, its fancy green ribbon and plastic wrap a chewed mess. She tossed it in the garbage.

I didn't consider it a major loss. It resembled Aunt Dottie's fruit cake I choked down every year at our holiday party so she wouldn't feel bad.

Quigley continued licking his mouth and cleaning his paws.

I smiled. "Well, at least now you know how to motivate him to model the merchandise." I eyed Quigley. "And you should appreciate the knit caps your mommy makes for you." I told the cat and Zoe about the bird stealing my knit beret.

Zoe laughed. Quigley curled up and went to sleep.

෨ఆ ఆ෨

On our drive home from the Christmas market, Declan texted that he'd been unable to find an open tire shop, so he was driving home on the spare. That sounded suicidal on these treacherous roads. I'd hoped he'd be there for my visit with the local historian, Nicholas Turney. Our passion for family history was one thing keeping us connected. And if it turned out my Coffey ancestor was a murderer, I'd need his moral support.

The elderly man lived a mile up the road from Declan's parents. Jane insisted I wear her neon-yellow walking vest. It was either that or the red flashing Christmas sweater. The vest wasn't exactly stylish over my long green coat, but it helped break the strong winds. I met two vehicles the entire way, including the Guinness truck barreling past, heading to Carter's pub as if they'd had a run on beer. They likely had after last night's party. The thought of drinking still made my stomach queasy.

Nicholas lived in a whitewashed bungalow with splintered yellow paint on the door. A bunny lay curled up sleeping on a bed of weeds in a flower box under an open window, where the scent of fried bacon wafted from the house. The man welcomed me with a gracious smile for the bottle of mulled wine I'd bought him at the Christmas market. Nicholas led me into a small room where a fire burned in a black cast-iron stove. Dirty dishes filled a wooden stand in front of a chair facing a console TV. An old movie played on the TV's wavy green-tinted screen. Repairmen probably didn't know how to fix the antique. Ireland history and genealogy research books trailed from shelves onto chairs and the wooden floor.

I gestured to several books he'd authored. "Looks like you've been doing this awhile." I slipped off my vest and coat and draped them over the back of a worn tan leather chair.

"Was a history professor at Trinity. Dabbled in genealogy when I taught and took it on as a full-time hobby after my retirement."

What a great feeling, touching so many lives, helping people learn about their pasts and find closure when needed. Although I helped people create memories that would last a lifetime, it'd be more fulfilling to do something that transcended a lifetime and lived on forever.

He lowered the volume on the TV. "Was a favorite of my wife, Annie's. We watched it every Christmas. *The Dead*." A somber expression replaced his kind smile.

"That doesn't sound real festive," I joked, trying to lighten the moment.

The holidays were a tough time to be without loved ones.

He laughed. "Suppose not. Become a bit of an Irish version of *The Christmas Carol*, it has. About reflecting on one's ghosts of Christmas past, present, and future. The short story was written by our own James Joyce."

I wasn't about to admit I'd thought James Joyce was English, not Irish.

"Set in 1904 Dublin."

"Twelve years before my grandma was born here."

However, the party being held on TV at the home of two older ladies was much more lavish than my rellies could have afforded. The room was larger than Grandma's house.

Nicholas fished a large manila envelope from the sea of papers on his desk and sealed it. "Need to pop this in the post before it goes missing. An Australian couple was in the area researching their ancestors, so I offered to see what info I might have and send it along. The local B and Bs often refer guests."

"Do you ever conduct research in Scotland?" When Bernice and Gracie sent me their family info, I'd have no clue where to begin.

"My research often leads me to Scotland and England."

"I'd appreciate a few pointers. I'm helping some friends with their Scottish family tree."

He selected two books from the shelves and handed them to me. "These should help. They're quite recent, include websites and such."

"Thank you so much. I'll mail them back to you."

"No worries, luv. You can return them next time you cross the pond." He gave me a wink. He lifted a jagged rock weighting down a copy of a newspaper clipping. "From my grandparents' home."

A stone from Grandma's childhood home would have made an even better souvenir than my Coffey pin.

He handed me the article on the attempted murder

of the landowner J. P. Daly and the murder of his sister. I scanned it.

"Your Coffey rellie isn't mentioned. If you were wondering."

"That's good. I'm not sure if they even lived there at that time."

"Would have to check the land records."

Or ask Sadie Collentine. I'd have to send her snail mail since she didn't have e-mail.

"Do you know who lives in the Daly house now?"

He shook his head. "You could check with the postmaster."

Declan had suggested the same thing.

"According to the article, J. P. Daly had a reputation for being a fair landlord. He'd given a man many chances before issuing an eviction notice. However, violence and unrest had peaked over the land wars. Although, the papers had slanted views, as they do today."

Out of the corner of my eye, I caught movement by the door. I glanced over to see a small, furry white butt scamper behind a bookshelf. Omigod. Mice scared the crap out of me. I was unsure if I should bring the critter to his attention or ignore it, not wanting him to be embarrassed that I might think his house was infested with rodents.

Nicholas slipped on a pair of wire-framed glasses and opened to a paper-clipped page in a worn, soft-bound booklet. "About thirty years ago, I transcribed the local cemeteries. There's a Richard and Emily Daly buried in one. The 1911 census lists them living on the Daly estate in Killybog with sons James and Richard, no John. And no John is buried in their cemetery plot. If they followed the Irish naming pattern, the firstborn James would have been named after Richard's father, J. P., and the second son would have been named after the mother's father. However, her father may have been Richard, same as her husband." He shook his head at the craziness of it all. "This naming tradition made for many identical first names, making research even more challenging."

"So it doesn't appear my grandma's husband John lived next door to her."

"Ah, there you are." Nicholas's gaze darted to the stand of dirty dishes, where a white furry butt stuck up from a bowl. "Didn't think you were going to stop by to do the dishes today."

The animal's head popped up from the bowl, whiskers and nose twitching, gravy covering the tips of its pink ears. The bunny from the window box, not a mouse.

"Meet my friend Stewey."

Stewey's head was back in the bowl, slurping up gravy.

It made me feel good that the man had a regular visitor.

"Now back to John," Nicholas said. "He mightn't been born yet."

"I'd kind of ruled it out anyway since they were married in Dublin."

"Rule number one in genealogy research, never *rule* anything out. Keep an open mind. Your grandmother living next to the Daly family could be coincidence or may not. John may have been a relative. Rule number two, know what to let go of and what to hang on to from the past. Don't let the past hang on to you." He handed me a stapled packet of papers. "A list of several dozen John or J. Dalys born from 1910 to 1916 in the Dublin and Killybog areas."

I scanned the three pages. "That's a lot of Johns."

He nodded. "Both John and Daly were very common names."

"So I've heard."

"I ran it from the civil registration database online. You'd have to go to the registrar's office to obtain a certificate with parents' names, for a fee."

I heaved a defeated sigh.

"Genealogy research requires much patience and perseverance, luv. The road to heaven is well signposted, but it's badly lit at night."

I didn't have time to be patient. I was leaving Ireland tomorrow. Despite my determination, I might have to accept that I'd be returning home without answers to Grandma's past.

CHAPTER FIFTEEN

My pace slowed at the sight of Declan's car sitting in the drive, a spare tire on the front passenger side. The nervous flutter in my chest intensified as I neared the house. Had Declan noticed our redecorating, besides the outdoor décor now being inside? If his family and he were sitting around the kitchen table discussing Shauna, I shouldn't intrude. Yet it'd be awkward to wait in the car for a few hours.

Wouldn't it?

Taking a deep breath, I stepped inside. The smiling wooden Minions greeted me in the foyer, and laughter, rather than crying or arguing, carried from the living room. I hung up Jane's yellow vest and my coat. I slipped off Zoe's muddy duck wellies, glancing up the stairs at the empty nail on the wall.

The picture was gone.

My stomach dropped.

At least I knew Declan's reaction.

I entered the living room, now known as Whoville,

housing the wooden village square and character figures. Jane, Zoe, and Declan sat sipping mulled wine. Quigley lay in the Grinch's sleigh in the middle of the room. I discreetly glanced over at another empty nail on the wall. Had Declan also taken my painting from the dresser? I wanted to demand he put them back. Wasn't Jane upset? Why hadn't she made him leave them? Maybe she hadn't noticed they were gone.

Stay calm.

I smiled at Jane. "I hope you guys haven't been waiting on me. It took a bit longer than expected."

"No worries. Colin won't be home for a few hours."

"And then we have a surprise," Zoe said.

"What?" I asked.

"A *surprise*." Declan's teasing smile didn't hide the uneasy look in his eyes.

The only open spot was on the couch next to him. I debated sharing the sleigh with Quigley, but the cat was sprawled out, hogging the entire seat. I sat on the couch, leaving plenty of room between Declan and me.

"Declan was just telling us about the fox he swerved to miss and the pothole that blew his tire," Zoe said. "It could have been a wicked accident."

"He could also have had one driving home on that tiny tire," Jane said.

"Shops were already closed for the holidays." Declan handed me a glass of wine, his fingers grazing mine, causing my breath to catch in my throat.

Don't cave!

"How'd it go at Nicholas Turney's?" he asked. "He have any new info for ya?"

I took a sip of wine, trying to relax. "The Dalys next

to my grandma's in the 1911 census were Richard and Emily, with sons James and Richard, but no John. Nicholas gave me a list of several dozen John Dalys born in Killybog and Dublin, 1910 to 1916."

"The registrar's office is closed for the hollies," Zoe said. "My friend Siobhan works in the building."

"I can go after," Declan said. "Shouldn't cost just to have a look. If I find any Johns with parents Richard and Emily, I'll pay the fee."

I gave him an appreciative smile.

"A nice man that Nicholas, isn't he?" Jane said.

I nodded. Everyone acting so pleasant made me want to scream out Shauna's name, forcing us to discuss what had happened. I took a gulp of wine.

Apparently sensing my tension, Zoe and Jane exchanged glances and stood. Not obvious at all.

"We'll get some snacks," Jane said as they fled the room.

Declan set his wine on the table. He moved closer to me, raising his arm. Instead of slipping it around my shoulder, he propped an elbow on the back of the couch, peering over at me. If I stared into those blue eyes, I'd be a goner, so I focused on my finger tracing the rim of the wineglass.

"Sorry about all of this. My tires are shite. Need new ones."

He was apologizing for shite tires?

"Where'd you go?"

"Over by Galway."

My gaze darted to his. "Isn't that on the West Coast?"

He nodded hesitantly, glancing away.

"You drove hours before you got a flat and had to stop for the day?"

He peered back over at me. "Sorry. Let's just forget about all of this. I don't want to ruin the rest of your visit."

No way was I forgetting what had happened. Jane and Zoe weren't going to let it go, were they? If they didn't say something, I would. Then *I'd* be the one ruining everyone's Christmas once again, not Declan. Yet I couldn't ignore everything that had happened between Declan and me, and also between Jane, Zoe, and me. I was so certain I was reaching them. I didn't want the lonely nails on the walls to once again speak for everyone, or rather, *keep* them from speaking.

Declan changed the topic, rambling on with ideas for researching John Daly. His enthusiasm seemed genuine, yet I seethed, my breathing becoming heavier. He was the master of avoidance. I took a drink of wine, trying to remain Zen rather than flying off the couch in a fit.

Zoe and Jane returned with more mulled wine and a tray of Minion-shaped sugar cookies decorated in green overalls and red Santa stocking caps.

Jane smiled brightly. "Fancy some cookies?"

I forced a perky smile. "They look delish." Instead of sticking my foot in my mouth, I stuck a cookie in it.

How many cookies would it take to keep me from saying something I regretted?

❧ ❧

Red ornaments decorated a small tree on the marble altar, and evergreen wreaths with gold bows hung from the arched stained-glassed windows. I entered Killybog's church, imagining Grandma and her neighbors sitting in the wooden pews, wishing each other a Happy Christmas, children squirming, anxious to get home to play with their presents. What had been Grandma's favorite gift? Had her parents been able to afford presents, or had the holiday been more about joining rellies after church for a festive dinner with potatoes, ham, turkey, and Christmas pudding?

"You look lovely," Declan said, placing a hand on my lower back.

Between Declan's gentle touch and his thoughtful surprise—mass at Grandma's church—I wanted to ignore everything that had happened the past few days. If I addressed Declan running off and refusing again to discuss Shauna, he'd get upset, and things between us would change. Was that why he'd brought me here? To soften me up? I feared it was working...

Declan's hand guided me from the doorway and into the church, allowing his family to enter. My black heels clicked against the tiled floor, echoing through the quiet church. The few dozen people occupying the wooden pews hugged the outer aisle by the wall registers. They were going to have to pray a bit harder for heat—the place was freezing. Declan directed me into a pew. Colin and Jane sat in front of us, Zoe ahead of them. If the registers kicked in, we'd have optimal seating.

Despite the chill, I slipped off my coat with Declan's assistance, wanting to show off Zoe's deep-purple velvet dress and purple lacey hat. Zoe had secured it in place with pins, yet I kept my shoulders squared and chin up, as if I had to balance it on my head or it might fall. It reminded me of when Rachel and I used to walk around the house balancing books on our heads, hoping to develop the posture of beauty pageant contestants.

Rather than telling me I was mad for removing my warm coat, Declan lay it in the pew next to him. He kept his long dark coat on over his dapper navy suit and blue shirt and tie. We were overdressed compared to others in jeans or casual dress slacks, who were likely saving their Sunday best for Christmas mass. I didn't feel overdressed for long. The five older men from Molloy's pub filed in wearing the same dark suits as the other day. Maybe daily mass was their excuse to hang out at the pub.

Declan rested his hand on the side of his leg, his pinkie touching mine. His sly smile made my chest flutter. It was kind of nice, yet unnerving, sitting alone with him, like a couple, when I had no clue what we were anymore. I shoved aside thoughts of our relationship and focused on the fact that my grandma's family had likely once lined this same pew. Had Grandma and Theresa chatted about their new holiday dresses, wondering if the cute boy sitting ahead of them noticed? What had brought them to the church the day their picture was taken out front? From everyone's dressy attire in the photo, I assumed it had been a wedding. I should have asked Sadie if her mom's albums had the same photo of Grandma and her sister. Maybe it'd noted the occasion and relative names. It suddenly dawned on me that the photo was dated 1935. Had Grandma been married at that time? Had she still had a relationship with her family and been living in the area? Or had she returned for a friend's wedding?

The priest walked out a door and stepped onto the altar.

"Jaysus," Declan said.

Jane shot him a scolding look over her shoulder.

Declan leaned toward me and whispered, "He's the priest who kicked me out of that church a few years ago. He probably does mass at several."

Maybe the priest wouldn't recognize Declan. Getting kicked out of my grandma's church would not be a good way for Declan to earn my forgiveness.

CHAPTER
SIXTEEN

Even though the priest had recognized Declan when we'd exited the church, he hadn't mentioned their previous encounter. He'd shaken his hand, wishing him a Happy Christmas.

When we returned home, we changed out of our dress clothes and met in the living room to eat the takeaway pizzas we'd picked up. Colin hadn't commented on Quigley's new bed in the middle of the room or the other outdoor decorations inside. Even though Jane felt her husband could be a stubborn arse, he appeared to accept her quirks without question. I was sitting on the couch next to Declan, trying to ignore our arms occasionally brushing as we reached for pizza or wine on the cocktail table.

After we finished eating, Zoe snatched a present from under the tree. "Caity opens the first one since she's a guest." She handed me a small box wrapped in green paper, from Declan.

I unwrapped the book *P.S. I Love You* by Cecelia

Ahern. Everyone stared curiously at it. "Ah, it's my favorite movie," I explained, not wanting them to read anything into the title. I glanced over at Declan. "You already got me a present. You shouldn't have done this."

He smiled anxiously. "Look inside."

I opened the cover to find the title page autographed.

I hope you get your purple wellies. Cecelia Ahern.

He'd remembered my comment about wanting purple wellies.

While touring County Wicklow last program, I'd admitted having seen the movie a dozen times and wanting purple wellies to row around the lake with my friends. I hadn't admitted that I didn't have any friends.

"I waited in line over an hour at her signing in Dublin last month. One of the only lads there. You'd have thought Oscar Wilde had risen from the dead to do a book signing."

I tried not to appear too touched that Declan had gone to such great lengths to get my present when he could have ordered an unsigned copy online and had it delivered to his doorstep. I'd be mortified if I'd given him the whiskey basket.

"Here, open our gift." Zoe bubbled with excitement, handing me a large box in snowman wrapping paper.

I opened it to find a pair of purple wellies. "Wow," I muttered, fighting back tears. "Thanks a mil."

"Thanks a mil?" Zoe laughed. "You're starting to sound Irish. Try them on."

I slipped on the boots and modeled them. They fit perfectly.

"They're lovely," Jane said. "Declan told us he was getting you the book and suggested the wellies."

"Next time you're here, we're renting a boat on Blessington Lake," Zoe said. "Hopefully, we don't lose our oars like in the movie. I've never rowed a boat before."

I smiled. "Neither have I."

"We'll make quite the pair."

Having a friend to go boating with was one of the best Christmas gifts of all.

"Everyone already thinks *you've* lost your oars," Declan told Zoe.

"Be nice or no pressies." Zoe teased Declan with my gift before handing it to him.

I nibbled nervously at my lower lip. What if he didn't like it? Or didn't get it?

He unwrapped the ornament. A dancing leprechaun smiled up at him. Declan peered over at me, a reminiscent glint in his eyes. "Ah, it's grand. Thanks."

I stared into his dreamy blue eyes for several moments before finally dragging my gaze away to share the story of my leprechaun socks with everyone. How I'd tripped in front of the VIP and Declan had come to my rescue for the first time.

He hung the ornament next to the one he'd painted with Santa in the orange suit. My smile faded. Next Christmas, would he choose not to hang it on the tree, reminded of me and our brief relationship? Like the lonely snowman ornament hid away in the box upstairs?

Zoe snatched up a round box wrapped in red paper with a gold bow. "Nice wrap job."

"Save Declan's present for when Aidan gets home," Jane said.

"I can't wait." Zoe tore off the paper and tossed the box top aside. She removed a fancy, small red hat with a cluster of red maple leaves on one side. She stared at it in awe. "It's the one Kate wore to the queen's River Pageant and on her visit to Canada."

"Not the *exact* same one, or that'd have set me back several quid, but I did buy it in London."

Zoe's eyes watered. "This is the most lovely gift ever. I can't believe you bought me something so…nice."

"What were you expecting? A hat with a bobblehead Kate on top?"

"Yeah." She gave Declan a huge hug. "Does this mean I have to start buying you proper gifts?"

"It means you two have grown up," Colin said.

"I thought it would be appropriate for the St. Stephen's Day races in Dublin," Declan said.

"I'm wearing it right now and never taking it off." Zoe placed the hat on her head, balancing it in place without the help of pins.

Jane opened my gift—a nutcracker missing its handle with the mouth. A clearance item from the Christmas market.

She eyed the wooden figure. "Ah, it's brilliant, isn't it? A nutcracker unable to crack nuts." She smiled appreciatively. "Been here just two days and you know me so well."

"Not going to cry over that yoke, are ya?" Colin asked.

"I'm getting misty because Caity's leaving." She peered over at me. "It's been lovely having ya here."

I swallowed the lump of emotion in my throat. "Thanks for opening my presents early. It was wonderful being included."

"Yeah, it's been nice," Declan said, smiling.

It'd been nice? He'd been gone half the time.

Zoe opened the Christmas pudding I'd snuck off to buy after Quigley ate ours, and Colin loved his bottle of mulled wine.

After we finished opening gifts, Zoe stood slowly, balancing the hat on her head. "I'm going to wear my hat to bed. Good night, my adoring public." She strolled gracefully from the room with a refined wave.

Jane placed a hand to her mouth, stifling an exaggerated yawn. "Yes, it's time to turn in. We want to be up early to wish Caity a safe trip." She and Colin headed upstairs.

Everyone undoubtedly assumed Declan and I needed to talk. I focused on my book cover and not on the nervous feeling fluttering around my stomach and chest. The bedroom doors shut. I slowly raised my gaze to Declan's. With a steamy look in his blue eyes, he grasped hold of my hand, drawing me closer to him on the couch. I didn't want our first kiss since Dublin to be a make-up kiss when we hadn't yet had an argument and resolved our problems. However, when he lowered his head and gently brushed his warm lips against mine, I went weak, relaxing back against the couch. It felt like two *years* rather than two *days* since we'd kissed. He leaned in for another kiss.

I peered over his shoulder at the empty nail on the wall. "I can't do this." I slipped around him and popped up from the couch. "I can't pretend like nothing happened. Like I didn't say Shauna's name. Like it didn't upset you so much you ran off for an entire day."

Declan stood. "Sorry. I hadn't planned to be gone so long. And it's okay. I know you didn't say her name on purpose."

My gaze narrowed in disbelief. "I'm not sorry that I said *Shauna*. Someone needed to say her name."

He inhaled a deep breath, then slowly eased it out. "Please don't do this now, Caity." Using my name reinforced his serious tone.

"Then when? Tomorrow morning when you're taking me to the airport? After Christmas, when I won't even be here?" *Tone down the anger and sarcasm. Act rational.* "When, Declan?"

He dropped his head back, letting out a frustrated groan. "Jaysus. I don't know." He tossed his arms up in the air. "Sometime. Just not *now*."

Screw rational. I wanted to grab his sweater and shake him senseless, but he was already senseless.

"You're not the only one still mourning Shauna." I felt like *I* was even mourning Shauna. I hadn't known her personally but had come to know her better over the past few days, and I felt the family's pain, not merely Declan's. "It took your mom three years to hang a picture back on that nail and put your painting on the wall." I gestured to the nail by the fireplace. "I can't believe you took them down."

His gaze narrowed in confusion. "What are you talking about?"

"Your painting that was hanging there."

He looked truly baffled.

My stomach dropped.

He hadn't taken down the picture or the painting.

His mom had.

I'd thought that blurting out Shauna's name had helped Jane take the necessary steps toward healing. She'd seemed so determined to move forward. What happened to that dark cloud hovering over the house for three years finally passing?

Declan eyed me with curiosity.

"Your engagement picture on the stairway wall has been stashed away for three years," I said, refusing to let it go, even though it was Jane's place to bring it up, not mine.

He quirked a brow. "How do you know about that?"

"Certainly not from you. Everything I've learned about Shauna is from your family, and that's not right."

Maybe destiny hadn't brought me here to help Declan or his family let go of the past. But to help myself. Martha would tell me that you couldn't help someone who didn't want to be helped. That it was difficult when you wanted something for someone more than they wanted it for themselves.

Declan's gaze narrowed. "What exactly have they been telling you?"

I shrugged. "It doesn't matter. Even if you don't want to talk about Shauna, you at least need to be able to say her name. To talk to her brother, Liam. Or to talk to *me* about Liam. To not drive off in a fit and go MIA for a day."

"They had no right to get involved in our relationship."

"*I* involved *them*. I told Zoe about our kiss and your mom that you admitted avoiding your emotions."

"Feckin' A, Caity." He raked a frustrated hand through his hair.

"They needed hope. *I* needed hope. That you'll learn to not live in the past so you'll have a future." Deciding I was on a roll, I added, "And I accidentally told Rachel about Shauna."

He didn't look surprised. Either he was overwhelmed by my confessions or he'd heard me in the restaurant's bathroom.

"I refuse to keep things bottled up inside like I used to. I want a relationship, but you're still in one, and I'm afraid you always will be."

I snapped my mouth shut, unable to believe I'd just said that. Declan looked just as shocked.

He shook his head. "As if it's so easy. You don't know what it's like to lose someone you love."

"Yeah, I do," I muttered.

I just lost you.

I turned and escaped up the stairs in my purple wellies.

CHAPTER SEVENTEEN

A loud shrill jarred me awake. My phone lit up on the nightstand like a beacon in the dark room. I shook the groggy haze from my head and snatched it up. It wasn't Mom forgetting the time difference and calling at 3:00 a.m.—it was the airline, advising me that my flight had been canceled.

Again?

I shot up in bed. I flipped on the lamp and almost screamed, startled by the wire sheep staring me in the face. My stomach dropped as I read the text informing me that my flight was rebooked for Christmas day!

I was going to have to spend Christmas with two hundred strangers flying over the Atlantic, dining on peanuts and swill wine while watching sitcom reruns. Even more upsetting, I'd be spending another day at Declan's.

No way was I staying here another day.

Declan didn't have to know my flight was canceled.

How was I going to keep that a secret when I didn't have a car? And, I had nowhere to go...

Yes, I did.

I needed to return to Grandma's home for a souvenir stone. To go to the post office and get the address for the woman who lived in the Daly home. Even if she wasn't related to Grandma's husband John Daly, she or a family member might know about Grandma's past. Nicholas Turney was right. I had to follow every lead. There was a reason my flight had been canceled the first time, so I could meet the local historian. There was a reason it had been canceled this time. My journey here wasn't done. My visit to Killybog wasn't about Declan. It was about Grandma and my family history and my family's future.

My future.

Feeling inspired, I convinced myself that I could drive in Ireland. Mullingar likely had a car rental agency. Declan had been a crappy navigator. I didn't need him sitting by my side or to have my back.

It was time I had my own back.

Early the next morning, I hauled my suitcase down the stairs, my carry-on bag weighing heavily on my shoulder, even though it didn't contain Declan's painting. I'd left it sitting on the dresser, not wanting a reminder of him hanging in my bedroom. I hadn't fallen back to sleep after my 3:00 a.m. wake-up call. I'd gone online and reserved a car from a rental company in Mullingar. Now I just had to figure out how to get there without telling Declan and his family that my flight had been canceled. An icky feeling tossed my stomach. Over lying, facing Declan after our argument, and saying good-bye to him and his family. I was going to miss my talks with Zoe and Jane. But it would be too difficult to stay in touch with them when I had to cut ties with Declan.

I hadn't merely lost Declan but also his family.

Zoe waited at the bottom of the stairs in her blue flannel jammies and her new fancy red hat. Not a red maple leaf out of place, she apparently hadn't slept in it.

She frowned. "He's not here. I'll take you to the airport."

I set my suitcase on the floor. "Where is he?"

She shrugged. "Supposedly had something important to do but promised he'd be back to take you." She glanced at the clock on the table. We'd planned to leave *now*.

"I'm such a bloody muppet sometimes. Should have left everything on the walls."

I stared at Zoe in disbelief. "*You* took down the picture and painting?"

"I thought if he got upset about them, he might leave again and ruin Mum's Christmas. But if I'd left them, maybe he'd have said something and we'd have talked about what happened."

I shook my head. "He wouldn't have. He'd just have taken them down."

Good to know Jane hadn't hidden them away. Maybe I *had* helped her. And Zoe had good intentions.

Declan running off again reinforced that I'd made the right decision.

"I don't need him to take me to the airport anyway. I booked a train. But if you could take me to the station, that'd be great." I hated lying to Zoe, but if she discovered my flight had canceled, she'd insist I stay here tonight, as would Jane. They wouldn't want me spending Christmas Eve alone. I wasn't keen on spending it alone either, but I had to.

"It's insane for you to drive me all the way to the airport when it'll be a madhouse today. Besides, I've never taken a train."

"A train doesn't go straight to the airport, ya know."

"Yeah, I know," I lied.

"I'll get dressed, and we can talk about it." Zoe trudged up the stairs.

I followed the scent of fresh-baked scones into the kitchen. Jane was sliding a tray from the oven. She forced a bright smile. "Happy Christmas Eve day."

I smiled. "You too."

"I'm packing a few sweets for your flight." A baggie on the counter contained Minion cookies. "He left before I was up this morning, or I wouldn't have allowed him to leave."

I shrugged. "That's okay. We said our good-byes last night. I'll feel horrible if he doesn't come back and I'll have ruined your family Christmas, twice."

"Nonsense. You didn't ruin our Christmas. Declan might still be refusing to talk about Shauna, but the rest of us aren't, and that's a good thing. Thank you for that. And I'm putting both the picture and the painting back up."

I was proud I'd helped Declan's family. I usually sucked in emotionally intense situations, never knowing how to react. That's the reason I'd decided not to become a counselor despite my sociology degree and desire to help women like Martha had helped me. I'd wanted to be at least one woman's Martha. Maybe I'd been two, Zoe's and Jane's. My eyes glassed over with tears.

"Ah, come here, luv." Jane embraced me in a hug, then drew back. "I'm so sorry things didn't work out for you two. I truly am. But you're always welcome here."

"Thanks." I nodded faintly, knowing I wouldn't see Jane again. Saying a final good-bye was too difficult, so I said, "I'm bringing my sister, Rachel, over in the spring to visit our rellies and Grandma's home."

I'm bringing *Rachel?* I hadn't said *we* were visiting Ireland or that *Rachel* was bringing *me*, but that *I* was bringing *her*. I'd never have thought myself capable of bringing Rachel anywhere.

But I was now.

❧ ❧

Zoe zipped around a sharp corner, taking it too wide, causing an oncoming car to veer partway onto the grass. We encountered a car creeping along, and she flew past it, branches scraping against my window. I grasped the door handle.

Zoe glanced over at me. "Sorry about that. No worries. I've only had two accidents. Three if you count the time my tire blew. But only one was my fault."

As if that was a stellar driving record. I'd never had *one* accident.

"Just because my brother is a total arse doesn't mean I'm not coming to visit you on holiday and see the snow."

I smiled. "Most people prefer to visit Milwaukee in the summer."

"I hope there's a fierce blizzard while I'm there and the snow is to the top of the garage door and we have to tunnel our way out. If you're back to Ireland before then, we can go boating. Don't forget to bring your new wellies. 'So now, all alone or not, you've gotta walk ahead.'" Zoe's panicked gaze darted to me. "Feck. Sorry. I didn't mean you and Declan. I was talking about—"

"The movie *P.S. I Love You.*" I smiled. "My friend Ashley and I used to quote it all the time."

Zoe relaxed back in her seat. "That's my favorite line even though I bawled. The way her mum and her connected was bloody lovely." She teared up.

I nodded, my eyes glassing over. "Bloody lovely." Both the movie scene and this one.

I'd finally found a friend I connected with like Ashley.

Zoe and I sobbed, swiping tears from our cheeks. She pulled off the narrow road into a pub's parking lot to get a grip and avoid her fourth accident. With runny noses and mascara-smeared eyes, we peered over at each other. We burst out laughing. The last time I'd laughed so hard that my side hurt was over one of Declan's stories. There was no way I was cutting ties with Zoe because of Declan. I refused to lose them both. And a friendship needed to be built on trust and openness.

I had to confide in Zoe about my plans.

"I need you to keep a secret."

Zoe wiped tears of laughter from her cheeks, smiling. "Fab. I love secrets."

"I need you to drop me at a car rental agency in Mullingar rather than the train station. My flight canceled again. I'm not leaving until tomorrow. I'm going to do more research."

"That's too bad you won't be home for the hollies, but I'll drive you wherever you like."

Besides needing to conduct my rellie search on my own, I felt this insane need to drive. Like it was part of my spiritual journey in Ireland. Not just because Zoe's driving scared me shitless.

"Thanks, but it's family stuff," I said. "Stuff I kind of need to do on my own."

"I understand. Where will you stay tonight?"

"A hotel by the airport. I figure it's best to drive there as late as possible so there's less traffic and less chance of an accident. You can't tell Declan my flight canceled."

"Believe me—I won't. He doesn't deserve to know. One day he'll regret being such a complete arse and letting you go."

Yeah, he'd chosen to let *me* go instead of his past.

I'd taken Declan's advice and rented a tiny car so I

had more room on the road than in the vehicle. Yet, it was hard to tell precisely how much room I did have on the road. A good thing I'd taken out full insurance coverage, even though I was driving so cautiously a long line of cars and tractors trailed behind me. They shouldn't be going eighty kilometers an hour anyway.

My confidence faltered after I drove down every narrow road, searching for Grandma's house. I finally came across the cemetery where my Coffey rellies were buried and remembered the way from there. I'd driven past the turn twice, thinking the grass-lined road was a farmer's drive. I parked in the same spot Declan had, at the entrance to a field. I pulled my purple wellies from my suitcase and slipped them on.

My phone signaled the arrival of an e-mail. I'd forgotten to turn off data roaming. My new cell plan should cover all my internet usage. I couldn't believe I had service here in the boonies. Two e-mails had loaded. One subject read *You're a Winner* and the other *February Meeting*, undoubtedly Heather responding to my question about my cancellation fee.

Afraid to know how little pay I was going to receive, I opened the first e-mail to find big brown puppy eyes staring back me.

I'd won the Irish terrier?

I could barely take care of myself. I certainly couldn't care for a dog. Besides the financial aspects, what would I do with it when I traveled? Mom wouldn't dog sit. Speaking of which, I couldn't take a dog back to the States. Shouldn't the contest rules have stipulated that the winner live in Ireland? Maybe Bernice had lied about my residency.

The dog's soft brown eyes brought back memories of Esme, the resident dog at my hotel in Paris. The affectionate springer had greeted me every morning at breakfast and upon my return nightly to the hotel. I missed snuggling in bed with her...

I closed the dog's picture, cussing out Bernice. I e-mailed her and suggested she and Gracie give the dog to their new Irish hotties as a Christmas present.

The second e-mail wasn't about the canceled meeting in February. It was from a client of Declan's inquiring if I could work a Prague meeting that same month. I confirmed my availability and mentally added Prague to my list of firsts. Unable to contain my excitement, I Googled Prague castles. A photo popped up with a breathtaking view of a castle set on a hill overlooking an old bridge and fairy-tale city. Checking off another castle on my bucket list made me almost as giddy as the future paycheck. Declan was going to Florence, the Canary Islands, and Portugal in February. This would be my first meeting without him. Adding this first to my list was a chance to prove I could fly solo without him having my back.

I slipped my phone into my coat pocket. After struggling with the weight of the rusted gate, I finally pushed it open. Wet grass and mud clung to my wellies as I traipsed over to the ivy-covered house. I wiggled a small stone loose from the window frame. Two more dropped to the ground. I hopped back, afraid the entire house was going to crumble down. When it didn't, I picked up the stones for Rachel and Mom and stuffed them in my coat pocket.

I curled my fingers around my stone. Three months

ago, I'd never have dreamed I'd be visiting Grandma's childhood home. I had never traveled abroad. I'd had no job, no money, no self-esteem, no friends, no relationship with family, no desire to date, no hope for the future, and no courage to drive on the opposite side of the road.

Now, I had all of this.

Well, maybe not enough money to clear my debt, but I was paying bills and no longer hiding them in a desk drawer.

My grasp tightened around the stone. Was this how Scarlett O'Hara had felt when she'd clutched a fistful of soil from the ground of her beloved Tara, vowing she'd never go hungry again?

I'd never let my past hold on to me again.

Words of wisdom from Nicholas Turney.

I had to stop beating myself up about my bleak financial situation, guilt over not always being there for Mom, and especially about Andy. He'd made me a weaker person those two years we were together, but I was now stronger because of it. I'd had the strength to walk away from Declan. Ironically, Declan had helped me regain my self-esteem and confidence. I believed in myself and that without him I wouldn't take a step backward in healing. Grandma had had the courage to walk away from her life in Ireland and start over on her own.

I was a bit depressed about not being home for Christmas, yet in some strange way I felt like I was home, never having had such a strong emotional connection to a place. I peered out over the fields my family had farmed for generations, savoring the moment...spotting a dark car parked in the distance at the Daly estate.

Did it belong to the owner from Dublin?

If she was a relation, she'd likely know the family's history and if John Daly had been related. She might also still hate the Coffeys. What if she got upset about me dropping in unannounced on Christmas Eve day? From my experience with the warm Irish hospitality, she'd invite me in for Christmas dinner with the family.

If I was lucky, she wouldn't serve goose curry.

CHAPTER
EIGHTEEN

Ivy climbed the massive oaks lining the dirt drive. I imagined the Daly kids climbing these trees while growing up. In summer, the towering trees' thick leaves likely canopied the drive, forming a tunnel. Now their bare branches quivered in the wind, along with my knit beret hanging on the end of one. That frickin' bird must have dropped it there. My heart did a little happy dance. After several attempts, I jumped high enough to snatch it from the low branch. I smiled, slipping the damp cap in my coat pocket.

This was a good sign.

Yet a nervous feeling fluttered in my chest as I neared the Daly house. I glanced over my shoulder at Grandma's home growing smaller in the distance. Closed green drapes prevented me from peeking through the house's tall white-paned windows. No welcome mat sat at the front door. No sign of life except for the fresh tire tracks and car in the drive. A shiver crept up my back. I eased out a shaky breath, curling and uncurling my fingers several times before pressing the button next to the red-painted door. Rather than a low ominous ding-dong, no ring sounded inside. I pressed the button harder.

A few moments later, the door creaked opened, revealing a tall, refined-looking elderly woman wrapped in a maroon shawl. Her gray eyes gave me a wary look.

"May, I help you?" she asked.

"Yes, ah…" I cleared my throat. "My name's Caity Shaw. I'm related to the Coffeys who lived down there." I gestured toward Grandma's house.

Rather than slamming the door in my face, a smile curved her thin lips, and she opened the door wider. "Related to Agnes, were ya? Now there's a name I haven't heard in some time."

This lady's parents had obviously never threatened to drop her off at Agnes Coffey's if she was naughty. She appeared to have fond memories of my great-aunt.

"I'm her sister Bridget's granddaughter."

Curiosity narrowed her gaze, deepening the wrinkles in her forehead. "Well, this is a surprise, isn't it now?"

I nodded faintly, even though it wasn't a question requiring an answer. We stared at each other a moment before she stepped aside, ushering me in. Dark wood-paneled walls and floors made the entryway feel as damp and cold as outside.

"May I take your coat?" She apparently noticed my hesitation, and added, "Sorry for the lack of heat. Just arrived from Dublin and was about to light a fire in the sitting room. This house is a beast to heat, with fuel costs. My late husband, Charles, always told me to sell it, but I still can't bring myself to give up the family home."

"Did you grow up here?"

She nodded. "Born and raised in this house."

My heart skipped a beat. "You didn't happen to have a brother John, did you?"

"Why, indeed I did."

My mind raced with questions. I tried to organize my scattered thoughts, not wanting to interrogate the woman and scare her off.

"Come into the sitting room for a cuppa."

I slipped off my green coat, and she hung it on a rack next to a long black one. I went to remove my dirty wellies.

"Ah, that's an American habit, isn't it? No worries, the boots will keep the toes warm from the cold floor."

My dirty purple wellies made me feel even more out of place next to Emily in her proper black heels buffed to a shine. I followed her down an unlit hallway, trying to step lightly on a worn red runner covering the wood floor. Gilded-framed paintings of distinguished-looking men lined the walls. It was like strolling through an exhibit at a Paris art museum. A tarnished metal plate on a frame read *J. P. Daly*. The landlord who'd been targeted by the angry tenants and whose sister had been mistakenly shot. His dark eyes and stern expression raised the hairs on my arms. He didn't look like a kind or fair man.

Emily opened a large door to an orangish-peach room. I blinked back the daylight pouring in through the cream-colored drapes held back with gold-tasseled ties. She lit a stack of peat in a large white marble fireplace, which had to be a complete nightmare to keep clean. Yet despite a light dusting of cobwebs on the ceiling's white crown molding, the place was neat and tidy. More portraits filled the walls along with numerous paintings of horses, some with dapper-looking gents in red riding outfits.

"My father owned several racehorses. It's popular here in Ireland, ya know."

I nodded, recalling my winning bet on Paddy's Sassy Lassy.

"Please, take a seat." She gestured to a green velvet couch and matching chairs with ornately carved wood trim.

I thought of the three-legged chair on the dirt floor in Grandma's house.

I sat on the couch. A claw-foot wooden cocktail table displayed a silver tray with a matching silver teapot, sugar bowl, and creamer. Four red floral china cups and saucers sat to the side of the tray. I checked a teacup bottom. An English manufacturer.

Emily arched a curious brow.

I explained about Flannery's china company.

"Ah yes, I'm familiar with them. They have some lovely patterns." She gestured to the cup and saucer. "You must keep one in memory of your pilgrimage to your grandmother's homeland. They were my grandparents', J. P. and Catherine Daly's."

"Thank you." A nice addition to my growing collection. I nodded at the elaborate tea service. "Are you expecting company?" I felt bad for intruding.

She shook her head, pouring a cup of tea. "My son and his family couldn't make it until tomorrow. I'm delighted you're here." She handed me the cup. "So now, do tell me. Why *are* you here?" I apparently looked taken aback by her question. Her features softened. "Not *here, here,* as in my house, which is grand, luv, but why are you here in Ireland, at your grandmother's old home?"

"I recently learned she was from Ireland. She died when I was only seven, and I want to know more about her."

She accepted my answer, pouring herself some tea.

I took a deep, encouraging breath. "She was married to your brother John, wasn't she?"

"She was."

"I have their wedding photo taken in Dublin."

A perplexed look narrowed her gaze. She took a photo album from a table and paged through it, finding Grandma's wedding photo. "Is this the snap you're referring to?"

I nodded slowly.

"It was their engagement photo."

"We thought it was a wedding gown."

"My brother purchased it when he still had access to family money. He knew they wouldn't have the means once they moved to England."

"They lived in England?"

"By our relatives in Lancashire."

The marriage certificate I had was for a Lancashire church.

"He didn't go by the name Michael, did he?"

She shrugged. "He may have after he left home. Michael was his middle name."

I told her about the marriage certificate.

"I would say that was likely him. No longer caring to have anything to do with the family likely included his family name. It belonged to our grandfather John Patrick, usually referred to as J. P."

Thoughts of Grandma and John Daly standing at the altar in a cold stone church in England, the pastor's voice echoing through the empty building, broke my heart.

Emily gazed reminiscently at the flames dancing in the fireplace. "She was a lovely girl."

I stopped shy of sipping my tea, lowering my cup. "You remember my grandma?"

"Yes. Not well, mind you. I was a very young girl, much younger than John. But I recall how she and her sisters would play in the yard and climb trees, their laughter carrying up to our house." She smiled. "Oh, how I longed to go down and play with them. But, of course, a proper young lady had to worry about keeping her dress clean. And instead, I studied French and mathematics at that same desk there."

A writing desk sat in front of the window facing Grandma's house in the distance. I imagined Emily staring outside, wanting to go play. I couldn't recall Grandma's laugh as well as she seemed to. I wasn't sure if it was because I'd rarely heard her laugh or my memories were vague, having been so young when she'd died. However, like Emily and unlike Mom, my memories of Grandma were happy ones. Wearing her purple apron and drinking hot cocoa from her teacups.

Emily had lived in this stately home and envied Grandma in her tiny stone cottage. Had Grandma longed to live in this house and learn French? However, she'd married John for love since he'd known marrying her would cut off his cash flow.

"It was no wonder John adored her. He always had. Nobody could blame him. Except for my parents, of course." She rolled her eyes. "That feud had gone on much too long."

"Because of the land?" I asked.

She nodded. "And the attempted murder of my grandfather."

My stomached clenched. "The Coffeys were involved?" I muttered.

"In a sense, at least according to my grandfather. He was certain your ancestor"—her gaze narrowed—"whose name I don't recall, had witnessed the murder of my grandfather's sister yet refused to cooperate with the authorities or testify. Of course, looking back, one couldn't fully blame your ancestor, if he even had indeed witnessed anything a' tall. A person would have been reluctant to turn on his neighbors at such a time of unrest. My grandfather took his silence as condoning the deed."

At least my ancestor hadn't been directly involved.

"We were told from a very young age not to mix with the Coffey family, which of course made us want to do it all the more." A mischievous glint filled her eyes. "My mother once caught Agnes and me walking home from school together. I was deathly afraid of what my father would do, but she never told him. He was all about the wealth and prestige. Even when much of his land reverted back to the Irish, Father's attitude never changed. Didn't even allow his own son to be buried in the family plot."

"When did John die?" I felt a strange sense of relief that he'd died and hadn't abandoned Grandma for another woman or family money.

"Shortly after they married. From TB. Tuberculosis. Known as the poor man's disease at that time, which of course added salt to Father's wound that his son should die of such an *inferior* disease. They were living in Lancashire, where he's buried."

"How sad. She had no family there to comfort her after he died."

"Her mother wanted her to return home, but her father wouldn't allow it. She lived with her sister nearby for a short while before traveling to America."

"Do you know why she went there? Friends, family?"

She shook her head. "Sorry, luv. Don't recall ever having heard."

Mom would certainly be more understanding once she learned why Grandma had kept her tragic life in Ireland a secret. She'd be more sympathetic to her distant emotions and for not having been the most nurturing mother. It had been a survival tactic, after her family had disowned her and the man she'd loved died. Marrying into a wealthy family could have provided her opportunities for a better life. That was why the Irish had immigrated, hope for a better future. She could have remained near her family if they'd accepted her marriage. And in the end, she'd lost them all. No wonder she'd claimed they were dead.

They'd been dead to her.

CHAPTER
NINETEEN

Walking back toward Grandma's house, I scrambled to replay my two-hour visit with Emily in my head, frantically typing notes into my phone. I'd have recorded our conversation but hadn't wanted to make her uncomfortable. I planned to document our entire family history for future generations. Better they know the truth than to wonder the worst like I had, afraid my ancestor might have been a murderer. And I'd never have figured out John and Michael were the same person if I hadn't met Emily.

Upon reaching Grandma's cottage, I peered at the Daly estate in the distance, nibbling at my lower lip.

I had to call Mom.

With each ring my anxiety increased and my courage diminished. If I hung up, she'd just call me back. She answered. I started with what I hoped would be the bad news, that my flight was canceled.

"You won't be home for the party or Christmas?" Her voice rose an octave.

"I'll be home tomorrow afternoon."

"If your flight doesn't cancel *again*." She let out a shaky breath. "I'm sorry. I don't want to make you feel worse, getting all emotional. This will just be the first party you've missed, and you'll barely be here for Christmas. I hope you'll be okay there. You won't be spending tonight alone, will you?"

"No," I lied. "I'll be with my friend Zoe."

Luckily, she didn't ask how Zoe and I had become friends.

"Ah, I have something else to tell you." I paced through the long grass, my wellies squishing against the soft ground.

"What?" Apprehension filled her voice.

"It's actually good news."

"Thank the Lord."

Peering over at Grandma's house, I took an encouraging breath. My story began six weeks ago, when Rachel had discovered the ship's record noting Grandma's married status, yet she'd been traveling alone under the name Daly. And then the marriage certificate I'd found online.

"I didn't want to say anything at that point because the marriage took place in England, which made me question that it was Grandma. I didn't want to tell you until I knew for sure."

Silence filled the line.

"Mom?"

"My mother was married before?" she said in disbelief. "And never told us? I wonder if my dad knew."

I explained why she'd kept it a secret. That Grandma had married her childhood sweetheart next door. The hardships she and John had endured to be together. That they'd been married in England because their families had disowned them, so they were in essence dead to her, except for her sister Theresa. And she'd lost her husband to TB.

"Why didn't she share all of this with our family?"

"Keeping an emotional distance was a survival tactic."

"But if we'd known"—Mom choked back a sob—"it would have made things easier."

The gate creaked behind me.

Startled, I stopped pacing and spun around to find Declan standing there.

My heart rate kicked up a notch, my breathing quickening.

"Ah, Mom, I should go. Are you going to be okay?"

"I'll be fine. Thank you for...everything. I love you."

"I love you too," I said as I disconnected and, with an apprehensive look, turned toward Declan.

"I checked your flight and saw it was canceled. Since Zoe had supposedly driven you to the airport, I grilled her until she caved. She's a hopeless romantic."

Unsure how to respond to his *hopeless romantic* comment, I stared at him in silence, then blurted out, "John Daly was also Michael, and my grandma's neighbor, and husband. He died in England before she moved to the US. From TB. I just met his sister, Emily." I glanced over my shoulder at the Daly estate. "She owns the house now. She was young when they married, but she remembers my grandma..." Was I rambling on like a lunatic because I was nervous or because I wanted to share this exciting discovery with Declan?

An enthusiastic glint sparkled in his blue eyes, his stance relaxed. "Guess it was a good thing your flight canceled. Not just so I could say I'm sorry about last night and this morning." He took a few tentative steps toward me. "It took me longer than I'd expected at Shauna's parents. We had a lot to catch up on after three years."

My heart took off like Paddy's Sassy Lassy out of the starting gate. Struggling to rein in my shock and excitement, I calmly said, "How'd it go?"

"They still have our engagement snap up. As they should." He took a deep breath. "Liam, of course, mentioned seeing us at the pub. I told them you're more than a coworker." He stared at me with a hopeful expression.

I didn't know what to say or if I even could speak, with the lump of emotion in my throat.

"It was difficult."

I nodded. "I'm sure."

"But losing you would be more difficult. If I haven't already lost you." His confident tone vanished, and his eyes pleaded with me to confirm he still had a chance.

I'd convinced myself that Declan and I separating was for the best. Going to see Shauna's parents was a huge step for him. However, I'd thought our kiss in Paris had been a major step. I'd hoped things would change after that. They had. But not enough. What if this was the same way? Declan cutting himself off from his emotions was kind of how Grandma had cut herself off for survival purposes. And she'd spent her life distanced from family.

I'd been strong enough to walk away from Declan. I

had to keep walking, even though my legs were starting to shake. I steeled my emotions, needing to be strong one last time. "You must feel a lot better, having seen them. I hope things continue to go well. But I, ah, have to go. I want to get to Dublin before it's dark out."

Was I planning to go on foot? It wouldn't get dark for another five hours, and Dublin was an hour's drive away.

His eyes glassing over, Declan peered up at the snowflakes beginning to fall. If he cried... I didn't know what I'd do. So I headed toward the road, focusing on the rusted gate and the last time Grandma had walked out it. Had she regretted never returning?

"It was in London, at a posh boutique hotel with a tiny lift. We got stuck between floors, and my claustrophobic client thought stripping down to her bra and knickers would help her not feel so confined. The lift started moving, and I threw my jacket around her. The door opened, and three security guards and engineering stood there grinning..."

As usual, Declan's story made me smile, yet a tear slipped down my cheek. Should I reach for the gate or Declan?

"I'm falling in love with you," he said. "You're only the second woman I've ever felt this way about, and it scared me."

My heart thumped in my ears, yet I continued staring at the gate. Even if Grandma regretted leaving home and never returning, I doubted she'd regretted loving John Daly, despite all odds. I didn't want to regret walking out that gate and never seeing Declan again. And this time, my gut told me I wouldn't be sorry for telling a man I loved him.

I turned toward Declan.

He stared hopefully at me, a tear trailing down his cheek.

I didn't need Declan to make me happy.

But I *wanted* him to.

My gaze never wavering from his, I walked slowly toward him. I stopped inches in front of him and kissed the warm moisture from his cheek. I brushed a kiss gently across his lips, and his breath hitched in his throat. My lips lingered near his, and I whispered, "I'm falling in love with you too."

He returned my soft kiss with a passionate one, slipping his arms around my waist. We deepened the kiss and wrapped our arms so tightly around each other even a snowflake couldn't come between us.

I vowed to not let *anything* ever come between us.

COMING MAY 2018

My
Wanderlust
the Bites
Dust

The Travel Mishaps of Caity Shaw

Eliza Watson

AUTHOR'S NOTE

Thank you so much for reading *My Christmas Goose Is Almost Cooked*. If you enjoyed Caity's adventures, I would greatly appreciate you taking the time to leave a review on Amazon, Goodreads, or another site. Reviews encourage potential readers to give my stories a try and I would love to hear your thoughts.

Thanks a mil!

ABOUT ELIZA WATSON

When Eliza isn't traveling for her job as an event planner, or tracing her ancestry roots through Ireland, she is at home in Wisconsin working on her next novel. She enjoys bouncing ideas off her husband, Mark, and her cats Quigley, Frankie, and Sammy.

Connect with Eliza Online

www.elizawatson.com

www.facebook.com/ElizaWatsonAuthor

www.twitter.com/ElizasBooks

CPSIA information can be obtained
at www.ICGtesting.com
Printed in the USA
LVHW051716030919
629788LV00012B/1046/P